GW01390077

WHISPER MURDER

WHISPER MURDER

Marjorie Stiling 84

Marjorie Stiling

The Book Guild Ltd
Sussex, England

First published in Great Britain in 2002 by
The Book Guild Ltd
25 High Street,
Lewes, East Sussex
BN7 2LU

Copyright © Marjorie Stiling 2002

The right of Marjorie Stiling to be identified as the author of
this work has been asserted by her in accordance with the
Copyright, Designs and Patents Act 1988.

All rights reserved. No part of this publication may be
reproduced, transmitted, or stored in a retrieval system, in any
form or by any means, without permission in writing from the
publisher, nor be otherwise circulated in any form of binding or
cover other than that in which it is published and without a simi-
lar condition being imposed on the subsequent purchaser.

All characters in this publication are fictitious and any
resemblance to real people, alive or dead, is purely coincidental.

Typesetting in Baskerville by
Keyboard Services, Luton, Bedfordshire

Printed in Great Britain by
Bookcraft (Bath) Ltd, Avon

A catalogue record for this book is available from
The British Library

ISBN 1 85776 628 8

1

The girl was missing. After five days of intensive search, there were already some who feared the worst. Even to Lorraine Barclay, new to the area and most closely involved, the leafy branches of the trees as they moved imperceptibly in the summer air, seemed to whisper murder.

Helicopters throbbed overhead. She covered her ears. Down in the village, police were making house-to-house enquiries. And much nearer, within sight if she dared to pull back the drawing-room curtains, mounted police combed the scrubby open common for disturbed patches among the gorse and heather. Relentlessly they invaded the small fir copses, the beech plantations, and the dense pine woods that circled her glorious, newly-discovered common, ever watchful for a discarded garment, a dropped possession, or even a body.

Reluctantly she uncovered her ears. Her hands came forward like a robot's, perfecting equal folds in the long gold-velvet curtains, careful to let no chink of light into the room from that dreadful world outside.

She straightened delightful Capo di Monte figures with plumb-line precision, and rearranged vases of flowers picked from the garden at first light when she had dared to venture out, before yesterday's abandoned search was resumed.

She pummelled and replaced her embroidered chair cushions for the hundredth time, as if by moving her limbs she could halt her mind, forget the past, the present, and all the conjecture of what might lie ahead.

It was no use. As if tuned to action replay, thoughts of the past five days ran on and returned until her head ached with their haunting repetition.

1

But it was twelve days ago, the day that Jeffrey was coming, that for her this nightmare had really begun.

Thursday, 25th July, was going to be another glorious day. She decided she even liked the smell of fresh paint; it seemed symbolic of the new start that she and Jeffrey were going to make.

She fixed her bedroom window wide open, breathed the fresh-coconut scent of gorse, and sighed with content. Not another house in sight. Just a vast expanse of purple and gold, circled by trees. Beyond them in the distance, the sea shimmered in the July sunshine.

Turning away, she picked up the framed photograph of Jeffrey from the dressing-table, and pressed it to her lips as if it were his warm flesh and blood.

She missed hearing his voice every day, asking how she was settling in, saying he loved her. She was thankful her own phone was to be installed next week. Trying to use the phone box in the village at pre-arranged times hadn't always worked. But she had loved getting his letters.

She looked forward to hearing the latest news when he arrived. Had he settled things in London; sold his flat, and finally agreed the financial claims of his ex-wife? God! It was extortionate what he, the innocent party, was expected to pay!

She put the photograph down, making sure it was perfectly in line with a picture of her parents, and one of funny Aunt Jo with her hat askew, before going on to the spare room where the smell of paint was coming from.

She was eager to see the room's bare wood floor cleared. Cans dribbled with undercoat, pastel gloss and emulsion; stepladders, surplus wallpaper, the trestle pasting-table; she wanted them all taken away. But the decorator, mealy-faced in his baggy white boiler suit, was still packing his brushes.

She stood back in the open doorway, mindful of its wet frame. 'It's super!'

He glanced up, hesitant. 'Aw. It ... it's not too pale then?'

'No. Just what I've always wanted. Exactly right. Shell

pink. And the transfers! They're perfect.' She moved closer to look at them. 'Real Country Diary. So right for here!' She paused. 'It's going to be a nursery. Well ... one day, I hope.'

'Aw.' He hesitated. 'Nice.' He sounded awkward.

Awful to be so shy, she thought. Or perhaps he disapproved, knowing she was unmarried. He probably knew her mail was delivered with the occasional letter for Mr Jeffrey Croft, who hadn't shown up yet; they soon knew everything in a village.

She said: 'I love the frieze. I nearly chose Disney. I did consider Beatrix Potter. I love animals.' She examined her well-manicured nails, reflecting. 'But real animals. I didn't want a duck wearing a poke bonnet. Or anything distorted, like Mickey Mouse, or Pluto.'

She looked around the newly-decorated room again. 'I like animals as they should be, perfect, don't you?' She broke off, 'Are you all right? You look awfully pale.'

He shuffled his foot, as if there were grit under his shoe. 'Aw. I'm fine.'

'I'll make some coffee before you go.' He looked anaemic to her, not too well, almost preoccupied. 'Bakers are pale, too. I expect it's your job.' She waited a moment, hoping he was really all right. 'Painter's colic don't some of them get?'

He shrugged, giving her a shy glance from under his sandy eyebrows.

'I hope you won't. Might want you back one day.' She smiled mischievously, and fingered the band of brown ribbon that matched her shoulder-length hair and kept it back from her face. 'You know ... to do some touching up, after the sticky little fingers...'

He half smiled.

'What's your name, who would I ask for?'

'Aw ... Ginger.'

'Right, Ginger. I can remember that.' She smoothed her smart dress over her slim hips.

He cleared his throat, shuffled his foot and said with

3

apparent effort, 'Aw ... er ... d ... do you always live alone ... like they was saying down The King's Arms?'

She guessed they had probably been discussing her in the village pub ever since she arrived three weeks ago. Natural enough. News travelled. A young woman in the isolated house on the verge of the common. But this was the most Ginger had said in two weeks.

'Actually,' she told him, 'Mr Croft is coming today. Next month he's going to manage his firm's branch in Draymouth. Hardly ten minutes away.' She didn't bother to add they would be getting married. Ginger must be her own age, but she had never met anyone so gauche at nearly thirty.

'Aw,' he said. 'Nice.' He pushed back his white cloth cap and scratched his head of fine, silky-looking hair, the colour of weak brandy.

She paid little attention to the intense gaze of his pale blue eyes; she only noticed that his freckles stood out against the paleness of his skin like splashes of gold paint. Repeating her offer of coffee, she left him to clear up.

Passing the landing window she paused to mull over her good fortune. Hidden behind the distant trees she knew there were farms, and cottages, and riding schools. She had seen little Thelwell characters on their ponies, being led along the bridle paths by sturdy jodhpur-clad women. Sometimes there were magnificent hunters with men sitting tall and upright in their saddles, evocative of cowboys riding out their range.

Downstairs she made coffee. From the kitchen window overlooking the drive, she watched Ginger packing his cans into a shabby little van, securing a short ladder onto the roof with a rope which he fastened to the handle of the passenger door.

He came in and drank a mug of coffee in his usual silence, hypnotically watching her every move.

She said: 'You'll be here tomorrow to start outside?'

'Aw.'

'I meant the preparing. The windows. Scrape them down

4

and fill them in with putty or whatever, before you can get down to the painting proper?'

'Aw. Yes.' He seemed to be hunting again for words. 'I ... I thought perhaps Monday. My mother's ill.'

'Oh I am sorry. Of course. Monday. Or whenever you like,' she added with genuine sympathy.

'I expect Monday,' he said heavily. 'That's ... that's if ... I mean, that's if she's gone.'

'Oh Ginger, I am sorry; as bad as that?'

He put his mug on the table and moved towards the door. 'Doctor don't ... don't think she'll last the weekend. She's sinking. Only four stone.' He brushed the back of his hand across his eyes. 'She's only fifty.'

The comment was scarcely audible, yet to Lorraine it sounded like an angry shout that it wasn't fair.

Leaving, he said louder, 'Monday, then.'

She heard him slam his van door and drive off. So that was why he was so quiet. She liked people who cared.

Upstairs she admired again the result of his two weeks' labour; she wrapped the intense pleasure it gave her around herself like an invisible cloak. She visualised the room furnished with a drop-side cot, and feather-weight embroidered covers. Perhaps a nursing chair, beside a neat chest of drawers for tiny dresses and matinee coats; and a satin-lined basket to hold all the baby's bits and bobs, so that everything was kept in order; organised; perfect.

She had been afraid Jeffrey might not want to start a second family, considering the way his only daughter had turned out. Thankfully he hadn't been put off, even though Kim, in his ex-wife's custody, had been nothing but trouble.

Charitably, she sympathised. It couldn't have been easy for Monica, left to bring up such a difficult child alone, while Jeffrey was abroad on business so long. And again during his other six months away, reason best forgotten. Perhaps Monica had needed those diversions, those numerous boyfriends, to help her to cope.

Lorraine went downstairs. She prepared the evening

5

meal, and hugged the thought that soon she and Jeffrey would be together at last. Just the two of them.

After a shower, she dressed carefully, choosing a cream silk suit with a wide, soft belt that accentuated her small waist. She used little make-up on her good skin, aware that already the country air had brought natural colour to her fine-boned cheeks.

She brushed back her long brown hair, and had just secured it with a fresh band of matching ribbon when she heard Jeffrey's car.

From the front door she watched him reverse into the drive. His same old cream Triumph in its usual need of a wash, with an added roof rack stacked with belongings. Any view he should have needed through the rear window was impeded by luggage. She hadn't reckoned on his bringing so much.

Almost before he braked, the front passenger door opened. A fair, curly head appeared, and Lorraine stood rigid. Kim! It couldn't be true!

'Bet you're surprised to see me, aren't you?' The leggy creature in a minuscule leather skirt, T-shirt taut over young, newly developing breasts, bounded to her side. She said, 'I had a dirty great row with my mother last night. I decided I'd rather live with my father.'

2

Lorraine opened her mouth to speak but her voice was drowned. Kim shouldered a huge, still-blaring radio, and brushed past into the house without waiting to be welcomed.

Jeffrey! How could he! Lorraine watched him ease his long legs from the car. Their eyes met. He snatched her into his arms. 'Not now darling, please!' He kissed her savagely, silencing possible protest. 'It won't be for long, I'm certain.' He stood back to appraise her, his voice husky with emotion. 'You look as gorgeous as ever. It's lovely to see you.'

'When did you know?' She didn't mean to sound sharp.

'Last night. Monica rang.' He turned to the car, making a great business of getting a suitcase from the back seat. 'I had to go over. I couldn't make Kim stay, there'd have been murder.' He straightened up. Holding a case in each hand, he pleaded softly. 'What could I do? Please Raine, for my sake ... I *am* her father.'

She faced him squarely, seeing the anxiety that puckered the fine splayed lines at the outer corners of his dark eyes. 'Of course. I know. But it's one hell of a shock!' She tried to quell her bitter disappointment. 'It's so unexpected, Jeff. I only hope she'll like it. Me. Everything. I suppose I'll have to do my best.'

The fresh crab salad, prepared for two, was enough for three. Kim, at fourteen, was already figure-conscious. She looked at least three years older, Lorraine thought; Biro slim, she was going to be tall, like her father. There the resemblance ended.

Throughout the meal, Kim chattered about herself, and rolled her blue, almond-shaped eyes affectedly. She called her father Jeff ... er ... *ee* with such repeated deliberation, Lorraine knew it was a childish act to let it be known to whom, exactly, he really belonged.

Lorraine sensed Jeffrey's irritation. Her heart went out to him; he was handling Kim carefully, as if easing a foot into a new shoe. Was the girl interested in nothing but herself, her possessions, and what she jolly well told Monica? She hadn't bothered to look out of the dining room's large bay window at the pretty, hedged-in flower garden, nor remarked on the view of the common with the sea sparkling in the distance.

A large portable radio-cassette, a guitar, and an assortment of Kim's possessions covered the spare chairs. Various treasures spilled across the green Wilton carpet. 'That was a super meal, Raine.' Jeffrey put his crumpled napkin on the table. 'Kim will give you a hand while I fix her bed.'

'I don't know where anything goes.'

'Any excuse, young lady. Raine will show you.' He stood up.

'Oh do mind, Jeff ... er ... *ee*! You nearly stood on my latest album.'

'Then pick it up, it doesn't belong on the floor.'

Raine was glad he asserted authority. The room was usually uncluttered; just flower arrangements on the cherry-wood sideboard that stood the length of one wall, and matched the oval dining table and high-back chairs. Two dramatic sunsets, which she had painted in oils some years ago, hung over the open, brick-built fireplace, now modernised with a log-effect electric fire.

It took Jeffrey a couple of hours to lay a piece of carpet on the spare-bedroom floor, put up the camp bed he had brought, and to find temporary furniture; chairs for Kim's clothes, a small table, and a standing mirror. 'The decorator's done a good job here, Raine.'

She was glad he approved. Something of her own enthusiasm had waned. Kim obviously took things for granted.

At least she didn't complain of the smell of paint, Raine was thankful for that.

'Yes, a really nice job.'

She felt too sick to tell him what she had in mind when she chose the décor. She guessed he knew; who but a baby would warrant stencils of daisies, and Mary with her little lamb?

The thought momentarily fuelled her resentment. But she wouldn't make him feel guilty, however obliquely, for something that was not his fault. She caught her breath and bit her lip. The walls and wainscot were barely dry, and now two suitcases, a cassette player, a guitar, a badminton racket, carrier bags stuffed to overflowing, and bulging cardboard boxes were stacked heavily against them.

With an effort, she closed her mind; time to ask Kim to be careful when they knew each other better and had made friends.

Next morning there was not a cloud in the sky. Raine asked: 'What shall we do, Jeff? It's going to be warm again.'

She saw him glance at the third place she had set for breakfast. Damn. Was he wondering what would suit Kim? She said: 'It's your day; that's if you really must go back to London tomorrow.'

'I must. Still things to do. Someone to see on Sunday. The sooner I go...' He looked across at the view through the window. 'It'll only be for four days. I'll be back Wednesday. Latish.'

She poured coffee. 'We could walk over the common, explore the woods or drive into town. It's market day, Friday.'

She went to the kitchen to fetch fresh toast. Coming back, she suggested: 'Or we could look in at the docks; some interesting ships come in to Draymouth.'

'Let's walk.'

She dressed in sensible shoes, slacks, a blue cotton blouse and a matching head band. 'What ever time does Kim get up?'

9

'God knows.'

'We can't go out and leave her.' She resisted saying that late risers were a nuisance, they hindered her routine.

'You call her, Raine. She likes you.'

'I hadn't noticed. But I'm working on it. She needs understanding.' Raine didn't want to start off on the wrong foot. Would Kim resent being practically told it was time to get up? Would she think she was being treated as a child?

Upstairs, only Kim's hair was visible on the pillow. Gently, Raine touched her. 'Kim?'

Thick, bubbly hair, the colour of Demerara sugar, was shaken from side to side. A cross, muffled voice insisted it was only ten o'clock. 'Not getting up yet. Don't eat breakfast.'

Raine felt her pleasure threatened. She and Jeff couldn't stay out for long, this first day, leaving Kim alone in a strange house.

They walked in companionable silence across the common, leaving the yellow grit pathways for softer, turfy tracks. Bees buzzed noisily over prickly gorse bushes that smelled of fresh sweet coconut. Further on, under the beech trees, the ground was soft and springy. And in the woods filled with the refreshing scent of pines, they trod over lacy patterns made by the sun as it filtered through the candle-tufted branches.

Raine couldn't enjoy it, the edge had gone. All she could think of was that her plans had been shattered. When Jeffrey's hand on hers made her pause to look up, thoughts of what had happened detracted from the sight of tiny gold-crests making undulating flights from tree to tree, breaking the cathedral silence of the woods with their thin, high-pitched call, zee-zee-zee. She showed little pleasure, she was thinking, *What future with Kim?*

She felt Jeffrey's arm go around her shoulder.

He said: 'I've been thinking, Raine. I think I could get Kim into a boarding school. I think I know somewhere.'

She wondered if she was hearing right. It seemed already

they were so close he could read her mind. She hugged him.

He said: 'A bit expensive. But near London. She could see Monica. They'll make it up. They always do.'

'Jeff, that would be wonderful.' Last night they had discussed wedding plans. Now his proposal to send Kim to boarding school heartened her, she felt encouraged in her efforts to go on trying to make friends.

Her lighter mood lasted all day. After lunch on Saturday, Jeffrey left for London.

They had planned that she would try to contact the local vicar. Kim wanted to stay in the garden with her radio; it meant Raine would have to go on her own. She felt just a little guilty, leaving the girl behind. She had wanted to take her around, show her the village, and some of the beautiful surrounding country. But she couldn't force it. Kim seemed happy wearing permanent earphones.

Raine drove to the village; down the long narrow twisting lane between hedges overgrown with grasses, foxgloves and tangles of white convolvulus that brushed the sides of her red Ford Escort.

She must remember to buy a local paper – she had put an advertisement in to sell the car. But even if it appeared today she didn't expect much response. Most people would prefer to phone before travelling so far off the beaten track to view on spec. All the same, she had thought an advert worth a try. It would have been nice to sell before her new car was delivered on the 1st August.

She picked up a paper at the post office, and drove on.

The vicarage was a small detached house, with ivy-covered walls, diamond-leaded casement windows, and a neat, lawn garden. Finding no one in, she went on to the church and parked on a rough patch of road outside the black oak lych gate.

The church door was open. Inside, she adjusted her eyes to the cool darkness and the variegated light across the dark pews from three small stained-glass windows. Floral arrangements hung from lamp-holders suspended from the

11

vaulted beamed roof. She went towards the altar, her sandals intrusive on the patterned stone tiles. She tried to tread softly down the aisle.

She paused to take in the quietness. It smelt of age, a hint of damp, the mustiness of old hymn books, the build-up of wax polish lavished over the years on the ancient pews and the oak lectern and altar rails, all overlaid with the heady scent of freshly-picked sweet peas arranged in vases at the foot of the carved eagle lectern, and around the pulpit. To smell so fresh they couldn't have been there long.

She went outside. There must be someone about, the place was open, weren't country churches prey to vandals? She followed the path bordered with old yew trees, and looked around the well-kept churchyard.

A young man by a grave looked up and straight at her for several moments. As she approached, he turned away and walked in the opposite direction so pointedly she assumed he must be grieving. She mustn't intrude.

In those few moments she was struck by his good looks. He was like an old-fashioned film star, almost too handsome to be real. She sauntered on, thinking about his bearing, the proud tilt of his head, the neat brown hair.

Some of the plots were well-tended, with fresh flowers. Others, mere mounds numbered with round iron disks stuck in the ground. She was treading the narrow paths carefully when a high-pitched whirring broke the graveyard silence. It came from behind the church, where in the far corner of the churchyard a man was using an electric strimmer.

She edged her way towards him past a high mound of earth covered with a mat of fake grass. Pieces on the ground formed a carpet. The deep sides of the freshly-dug grave were lined with posies of violets and small white flowers hung onto fixed netting. She knew it was a country custom to camouflage the stark reality of raw earth, but she had not seen it before. She pondered on what love and tears and patience must have gone into such work.

She avoided treading on the long electric cable lying along the path. A thick-set man of about fifty glanced up, saw her coming, and switched off the grass-cutter.

'Afternoon, Miss.'

'Hello. I'm sorry to interrupt the good work.' He was sweating, had stripped off his shirt, but wore a big red 'kerchief around his neck. 'Would you happen to know where I can find the vicar?'

''Ave 'e tried the vic'rage?'

'He wasn't there.'

'You be a stranger, bain't you?'

'I've been here three weeks...'

He eyed her up and down. 'I knew I'd never seed 'e before.'

'The church door's wide open. Is there a verger or some-one?'

''Aven't got one proper. Not since ol' Charlie Green died. Anyway, tis Saturdee.' He wiped his red moon face with a big black handkerchief 'I gives eye to the church. I be Fred Palmer. General dogsbody. Looks after the yard mostly.'

'Don't you have a half day?'

He rubbed the back of his neck and returned the hand-kerchief to his baggy trouser's pocket. 'Nah ... rather be doin' me yard.'

'It certainly looks well kept.'

'Aye. Is an' all.' He sounded pleased with the com-pliment. 'Council puts in every yer fer prize fer bes' kep' village garden. But they don't do nought 'bout bes' kep' churchyard.'

She saw his pride as he looked around.

'There bain't nother yard, better kep', nowhere, I reckons.'

She supposed it was his dedication that prompted the strange look in his red-rimmed eyes, and the way his lips curled. She wasn't sure she liked him, in spite of his rich gravelly country burr. She said: 'I saw a young man just now. Tall and slim. I thought perhaps he was the verger.'

13

'Wouldn' be verger. Charlie Green's gone.'

'I was going to ask him, but he turned away.'

'I 'spect that were Bible Billy.'

'He seemed upset.'

''E weren't upset, maid.' Fred sounded derisive. His broad chest and shoulders glistened in the sun. 'Not if it were Billy, 'e weren't.'

'He looked like a film star.'

'Aye. That'd be Billy, all right.'

She wondered, by his tone, what he meant to imply.

'He saw me, and deliberately turned away.'

'Billy don't like maids. 'Fraid of 'em, I 'spect.' Fred gave a short laugh and wiped his sweating face again. 'Might corrupt 'im, see? Corrupt 'is thoughts if nought else. Mummy's boy. 'Er would never allow 'im to look at maids.'

'What's he doing here?'

'Communing with God most likely. Talking to 'is Master, Lord Jesus Christ. Everyone knows Billy. Us takes no notice.' Fred wiped his hands. 'The local maids don't give 'im time o' day.'

'Why's that?'

'Well ... I spose they thinks like a cow do avoiding a buttercup. They knows 'e be no good to 'em.'

'But he's so good-looking!'

'Blasted nuisance, good-looking or not.' Fred momentarily forgot his vouched reverence for his graveyard; he spat on the grass. 'Tacks 'imself on to funerals. Tells mourners where the souls of their loved ones be gone to.'

'I went into the church ... anyone could.'

'Aye. But bit o' air doos the place good.' He wiped the back of his neck. 'I locks up when I go, if there's nought going on. Or else Billy do. He do, mostly. I gives 'e the key.'

'Aren't you afraid of thieves or vandals, when you're all down here?'

'Us did 'ave 'em back along. Sev'ral times. Now Billy'd soon 'ave 'em, I reckon. 'E's always 'anging around. Never far away. Self-appointed churchyard watch.' Fred sounded

14

scornful. 'On the other 'and, if they come again, I reckons 'e'd probably be off like a long-dog.'

Fred bent down, picked up a large stone and hurled it at a stray dog. 'Shhh – get out of it you...!' His colour deepened. 'Just gonna do 'is business. I always keeps a stone 'andy. It's my churchyard. Mine! No one messes my churchyard!'

She flinched, glad the dog wasn't hit. There was no point in staying, she would have to see the vicar another time, with Jeff perhaps. Now she must get back to Kim.

On reaching home, she was surprised to see a blue car parked outside her gate, two men in the front. She turned into the drive, braked sharply and got out quickly. One of them also got out and walked in after her.

He was a swarthy man about her own age, in stone-washed jeans and white singlet. His thick gold necklace and large, hooped earrings made her think of gypsies, and he held a rolled newspaper.

'Afternoon, mam, I've come about the car. This right place?'

She smiled and indicated 'Yes. It's this one.'

He kicked the tyres, peered in at the upholstery, then walked to the back and tried the boot.

'I can unlock it.' She moved to get the keys from the ignition.

'No, don't bother. It's okay.' He examined the bodywork for rust, then opened the front door, pressed the button that released the bonnet. As he leaned over the engine she noticed his thick arms, tattooed with evil-looking snakes, green, scarlet and black, interspersed with fork-tongued devils.

He shut the bonnet. 'How about a trial?'

She felt suddenly nervous; a natural request she hadn't considered. Suppose he drove off and she never saw him again? The thought of accompanying him, alone, was even worse. Perhaps she had been silly to advertise, but she had thought Jeffrey would be here and she had so wanted to

15

get rid of the car before the 1st August. They hadn't really room to park three cars.

Uneasy, she watched him scrutinise the dashboard, the petrol gauge, the mileage. Kim wasn't still in the garden, or she would have joined them. Could she fetch Kim from indoors? Any moral support was better than none.

He considered a moment, then said slowly. 'Don't think I need a test. Saw you drive up, sounded okay. The price your lowest?'

She hated bargaining, was no good at it. But relief made her firm; she surprised herself. 'It's very good condition.'

'Okay,' he conceded promptly. 'Thing is, I'm off for a few days. Deposit do? Rest when I fetch it? Say next Wednesday?'

'Fine.'

'Be sometime in the evening.'

'That'll be fine. You can fill in the registration document for Swansea when you pick it up.'

He counted out ten grubby twenty-pound notes and went off without a receipt.

She couldn't believe it. He trusted her completely. It said much for him.

Back to earth, in light mood, she called Kim. They would go for a drive this evening, have a meal out.

Kim didn't answer and wasn't in her room. Annoyed, Raine tried to reason. The girl had a right to go out, but couldn't she have left a note? Where had she gone, and how long might she be?

Drinking tea, she wondered if she had passed Kim on the road as she drove home. Should she go back to look? Or would that cause resentment?

She tried to be patient. After three hours, unable to concentrate, her anxiety grew and slowly turned to anger, then to self-incrimination. She was responsible. She should have stayed in the garden with Kim and her wretched music.

It was getting late. She felt uneasy. What should she do? Drive down to the village? Look around, make enquiries? But if Kim had gone up the lane towards the common, there were so many paths she might have taken.

16

She kept going to the drive gate and willing her eyes to see a lank figure in a short skirt. As it grew dusk, her hopeful imagination made her see movements in the shadows of the overgrown hedges, that might be Kim coming.

Suppose Kim had lost her way? Or something had happened? Her stomach churned. How would she tell Jeff?

She had to do something; notify the police in Draymouth. If only she were on the phone.

She went indoors to fetch her car keys. Almost before she had picked them up she heard a car door slam. Moments later, Kim came in.

'Hi.' Kim peeled off her thin white anorak.

Raine felt her cheeks pale with relief. 'Kim! Wherever have you been?'

'Disco. In Draymouth.' She sounded defiant, pleased with herself.

Raine was annoyed by the anorak dropped onto the floor, and even more so by the girl's badly made-up face, but she made an effort to sound calm. 'Why didn't you tell me?'

'I can go out, can't I?'

'Of course, but I was worried.' Weren't those her own jade earrings Kim was wearing? 'How exactly...?'

'Walked down the lane. Caught a bus from the main road.'

'If only you'd said.'

'You weren't here.'

Raine saw through the excuse; Kim had waited until there was no one around to tell. 'Did I hear a taxi?'

'No. Some fella. I caught the last bus. Then hitched.'

'Have you eaten?' And surely that hideous lipstick was one of her own bad buys?

'I had some Coke.'

'What would you like to eat?'

'I would have had another Coke...' Kim's tone implied she knew there wouldn't be one, but if there was she would have done a favour by drinking it.

Raine picked up the anorak from the floor and put it

17

over the back of a chair. Kim slumped on to the settee, long legs outstretched, her skirt scarcely visible. There couldn't be many such jade earrings the size of an old penny with a Buddha in relief. It seemed too much of a coincidence that this girl should own a pair so exactly like those which Aunt Jo had brought Raine from Beijing.

'Are those my earrings, Kim?'

'Didn't think you'd mind.'

'I don't. But I'd rather you'd asked.' The earrings didn't matter. She had had a craze for jade once so everyone, especially Aunt Jo, had kept giving her jade. She had tired of it.

'You weren't here.' Kim defended.

Raine thought it best, for the moment, not to say that what she minded was Kim going into her room. Smiling, she said, 'And my lipstick?'

Kim rummaged in her large canvas shoulder bag.

A sharp pain shot through Raine's head, she gasped and recoiled, clamping her hands over her eyes.

'Keep your crumby old lipstick!' Kim shouted, and stamped off to bed.

3

Raine pressed her fingers to her eye. It hurt. Had she been too heavy-handed with Kim after all? Perhaps it was normal for a fourteen-year-old girl to be out until midnight, and to treat other people's property as their own.

She didn't mind about the earrings; Kim could keep them. But the lipstick was awful. Rose pink clashed with Kim's orange T-shirt. It made her look cheap. Raine would like, very nicely, at another time, to point that out.

She was thankful, next morning, to find Kim up early and in a better mood. With limited option of what to do, she actually agreed to go with Raine to church.

It was Raine's first attendance; she had been so busy since she had moved here, getting the house straight.

Inside the church door, she recognised the good-looking young man she had seen in the churchyard, yesterday, whom the grass-cutter had called Bible Billy. Solemn-faced, eyes downcast, he handed them each a hymn book and psalter.

Kim put out her hand but, with her thumb and forefinger around the books, she didn't take them. As the tall young man's eyes remained on the books, she slid her hand along until her thumb touched his, then she twisted her hand and smoothed the back of it against his wrist. Wondering, he was forced to look at her.

It seemed an eternity to Raine before he returned Kim's wide, brazen smile with a tight one of his own.

From time to time, throughout the service, Kim twisted around in the pew to look at the congregation. She smiled at a man just behind, and at another across the aisle. Then at every male whose attention she managed to catch, she rolled her eyes and narrowed them; calculating, teasing.

Raine's face burned; she wished she hadn't come. She couldn't concentrate on what she had expected to enjoy, and instead became ever more aware of the cool mustiness around her than the soporific voice delivering a sermon, and the scent of carefully arranged flowers throughout the nave.

Her attention wandered. She read some of the plaques on the thick, white-painted, uneven walls, dedicated to eminent local worthies and benefactors; and in memory of one Harry Joshua Perry, the verger who had served this parish faithfully for fifty years.

During the offertory hymn, Bible Billy appeared at the end of the pew with a collection bag to be passed along. Raine saw Kim fix her eyes on him. His remained downcast. Kim's gaze followed him down the aisle to the chancel steps, and watched him hand the offertory to the vicar.

Afterwards, outside, she hung around in the dispersing congregation. 'Where's that whacky guy got to?'

Raine wished she would keep her voice down.

'Who is that whacky guy?' Kim pestered all the way home. It seemed he had disappeared.

'You're wasting your time, Kim.'

'How d'you know?'

'He's not interested in girls.'

'How d'you know?'

'A little bird.'

'He didn't see me. He was busy.'

After lunch, Kim spread herself on the lawn, and spared herself the sounds of bees and the country by hooping the large earphones of her radio over her head.

Raine settled down on a canopied, swing garden seat, to read a book.

Soon Kim looked up; shifted the earphones. 'Don't know what to do ... there's nothing to do.'

'We could go for a drive,' Rained suggested. 'Have you ever been to Dartmoor?'

'Any discos?'

'It's lovely country; sheep and ponies roaming free. There's a beautiful river ... waterfalls ... and an adventure park...'

Raine saw Kim wasn't impressed, and guessed this was what Jeff meant when he said Kim wouldn't stay long.

On Monday morning, Kim asked, 'Where does that whacky guy live?'

Raine knew who she meant. 'I don't know, Kim.'

'If I go out, I might see him.'

'This morning, Telecom are coming to do the phone.'

'So what? I don't need you, do I, to go out?'

Raine flinched at the scorn; the rudeness; she had never met, let alone mixed with, anyone like this. 'I suppose not.' But she had decided, after Kim's escapade on Saturday, not to let her go off on her own again like that. Now, how could she stop her?

If only Kim would wear something different; she had plenty of clothes, yet lived in her favourite, tiny black leather skirt. In these parts, it attracted the wrong sort of attention. People stared.

Telecom arrived as promised. Later, Raine filled in her telephone number on some self-addressed cards, and put a couple into her bag.

She started to tidy the house, picking up a pair of yellow flip-flops from the middle of the kitchen floor where Kim had left them. She put them away tidily in a cupboard. Two discarded T-shirts belonged upstairs. She took them up.

It was against her principles to go into a room when it was being used by someone else, but she couldn't have Kim's clothes lying around the house all day.

In Kim's room, she stopped short. Kim's bed was made, after a fashion; all bumps, the bedspread mostly on the floor. The walls were covered with posters which, on closer inspection, Raine saw were adhered to the new paper with wide sticky tape.

21

Her blood boiled. Gently she tried to lift one corner of the tape and, as she feared, it removed the surface of the paper as well. Viewing the spoilt room with dismay, she was reminded of Ginger; he hadn't turned up. His last words had been, when they discussed his starting the outside painting, 'Monday, then.'

She tried to remember if his not coming meant that his mother had died, or if she was still ill. Whichever it was, she felt sorry. Her sadness for him, and her suppressed anger with Kim, were tinged with shame. There was a dig in the door where it must have received a hard knock, probably from Kim's unwieldy Sony radio; and there was red nail-varnish splashed on the wall beside the bed. She wondered what time Kim would be back for lunch. But the day turned out to be a repeat of Saturday. She waited all evening. Anxiously she looked down the darkening lane; all that appeared were a few distant lights down in the village.

The village of Drayford, off the main road to Draymouth, was little more than a single-track road, lined with small terraced cottages, each with a tiny painted wooden door that opened directly onto the street.

It straggled for about a mile, giving up its debatable old-world charm in an occasional side-turning where, cottages having succumbed to age, or courtyards or fields had been sold for development, a few incongruous new bungalows were going up.

To Kim, coming back to it on the bus after her long day in Draymouth, the village was like a good-time desert. No discos or cinema. You couldn't count the Drayford Family Stores, the tiny Post Office-cum-newsagents, nor the silly little baker's. They baked bread in proper factories where she'd come from; not in a titchy bakehouse behind the shop that gave out a warm, doughnutty smell. She hated that, anyway, because she liked doughnuts but couldn't eat them, they would make you fat. Even the low-ceilinged Tudor Café that claimed to serve cream teas, appeared to shut at five o'clock.

She wanted to find out where that whacky guy lived; behind which row of small, lace-curtained windows did he eat, and sleep, and lay his handsome head?

She wandered the length of the village. With a sudden lift of hope, she gravitated towards the village hall from where a buzz of activity came through its open door. She found, as proclaimed on posters outside, there was a whist drive in progress. She rolled her almond eyes and raised them to heaven. As she walked on, the occasional quaint street lamp appeared to light itself. Through uncurtained windows, in the corner of tiny rooms, televisions flickered like cats' eyes in the dark.

There was still the public house to explore; maybe he went there for a drink, what else to do in this dump?

On the way, she passed the foot of the lane that, with its busy, overgrown hedges of convolvulus and nettles, led up to the house on the common. She supposed Lorraine would be waiting up for her as she had on Saturday. Well, let her wait. She didn't care. She wouldn't argue when she got in, she would go straight to bed; who did Lorraine Barclay think she was?

There were few people about, but those that were, knew a stranger; after she had gone by they turned to look at the long-legged young creature in a minuscule black leather skirt.

Outside The King's Arms, a gang of rowdy youths stopped their horseplay as one of them saw her, nudged his mate, and each in turn poked his neighbour. As one, they swung round, and whistled.

Their attention pleased her. At any other time she would have been quickly among them; rolling her eyes, teasing their masculinity, intentionally rousing. But she wanted to find the whacky guy who yesterday gave her a hymn book in church.

Without stopping, she smiled at them over her shoulder, with a little cat-like widening of her almond-shaped blue eyes; a gesture she had seen someone do in a late-night movie on the telly, and she had perfected it for a long time.

It looked quite a nice pub, she thought, considering. Double-fronted, and sash windows of patterned frosted glass, the top half open.

Neon lighting spilled across the small forecourt onto beer-barrel tubs filled with begonias. There were rough wooden forms, and tables left empty but for thick glass ash trays filled with cigarette stubs, squashed-in beer and coke cans, and scrunched-up cellophane bags that had contained potato crisps.

She went towards the open door of the saloon bar hoping, for once in her life, that the guys wouldn't follow. She heard the raised clamour of convivial voices, and people laughing. She looked round the door; there was a saloon on each side, crowds standing round the bars. She couldn't see him, the place was packed. Perhaps she would come back nearer to closing time, there might not be so many. In the meantime, there was nothing left to see; no more houses; only the church, just round the corner. With nowhere better to go, she sauntered that way.

The church stood well back, but the wide, rough square of road that fronted the lych gate was in heavy shadow of The King's Arms on one side, and a high brick wall that enclosed the extended churchyard, on the other.

She wasn't keen on going into the dark patch; and the weak light bulb suspended from the ridged roof over the lych gate, only made the small area it reached, look eerie. She was about to turn tail for the lights of the pub, when she saw something. It moved; silently; like a ghost. A figure. Tall. Slim. A smooth head caught in the feeble light as it passed through the lych gate into the churchyard.

She couldn't believe it. It was *him*, she was quite sure it was him. She took a deep breath, began to run over the rough road, through the lych gate, up the path. She caught him up inside the porch. 'Hello.'

'Who?' he asked sharply.

She went up close to him so that even in the darkness of the open porch she could see his face dimly. 'I came to church. Yesterday. You gave me a hymn book. Remember?'

He cleared his throat nervously. 'Oh ... oh yes ... I think I remember. What are you doing here?'

'I wanted to see you.'

'Who are you? You shouldn't be here.'

'I like you.'

'You must go away. You shouldn't be here.'

'Why not? You are. What're you doing?'

'I've just locked up. Always late, Monday. There was choir practice.'

She liked his voice; it was rich; low, but clear; much nicer than that of the boys she knew, exactly right for his whacky looks; the sort of dreamy voice that turned her on. 'Where are you going now?'

He pocketed the church key. 'I always look around. See everything's all right; that there's no one about that shouldn't be.'

'Then where're you going?'

'Home.'

She put out her hands as he moved to leave; his chest felt warm through his thin shirt.

He moved her aside. 'Excuse me, I want to get my jacket.' He reached in the darkness to a peg on the wall. 'I left it earlier. I often do.'

She made futile and unnecessary efforts to help him on with it. 'Why can't you stay and talk?'

'I'm afraid I don't know you.'

'What's the matter? Girlfriend jealous?'

He stood with his back against the solid, carved oak door. 'I haven't a girlfriend. Now really, I must go.' Gently he took her hands from his chest where she had put them again and was moving them sensually inside his jacket. He placed them down at her sides.

'No harm in talking, is there?'

'No. But not just now.'

'You're afraid. You have got a girl, haven't you? She's waiting.'

'Oh no no no, there's no girl.'

'Why? Don't you ... don't you love anyone?'

25

'Oh yes. Of course. I love our Lord Jesus Christ.'

'I mean girls. Don't you love girls?'

'No! Now if you don't mind, please...' He stepped aside to move out of her way to leave the porch, but she moved with him. He said, 'Your mother will be worrying where you are.'

'She's dead.' Kim spat the words out as if the very idea was breaking her heart.

'Oh. I'm very sorry.' He leaned back against the door and for a split second gave her hand a reassuring squeeze of sympathy. 'Well ... whoever looks after you ... they might be worrying.'

'My aunty. She says it's all right. I can stay out as late as I like. It's holidays.'

'Oh. I see.' He paused. 'Well, I really must go.'

'Mustn't you, then?'

'Mustn't I what?'

'Oh go on. You know.' She pressed herself against him.

Gently he tried to ease her away. 'Please. Stop it.'

'Don't you like being touched?' But she had already heard his quick intake of breath, and felt his firm grip on her shoulders, slacken. Instinct told her this was the moment to appeal for his sympathy, and to his sexuality. 'I'm sorry. I can't help being loving. But I don't know anyone here. I've got no one to talk to.'

'Oh. I am sorry. Then I will pray for you. And our Lord Jesus will comfort you.'

She pressed harder against him. Desperately, in the moments before she was afraid she might feel him push her away again, she appealed, 'Please! Can't You? Can't you comfort me? Stay and talk. *Please!* Go on. Just for a little while.'

4

When Kim eventually arrived indoors, she avoided any confrontation with Raine in the way she had been determined. She refused Raine's concerned offers of food and drink, and went straight to bed.

Raine had long since tired of watching the dark lane, and the village lights in the distance. She took comfort from the thought – only two more days. Then Jeff must take responsibility.

But she didn't sleep well. She was up early next morning, long before she heard Ginger arrive outside the kitchen window.

With considerable clattering, he drew an extended ladder from the roof of his van and propped it against the wall.

She opened the back door. 'Good morning.'

'Aw. 'Morning.' He hesitated, then came nearer. 'She passed away. Early Monday. Yesterday.'

'Oh, I'm sorry, Ginger. I *am sorry*.' She wanted to spare him explanation. 'It's good of you to come. There's no need if you would rather...'

'Aw. I can ... can do today all right. An' tomorrow. Not Thursday.'

She was surprised by the look in the pale blue eyes that met hers. Was it eagerness to work, as a catharsis for his loss? 'Well ... only if you're sure.'

He shuffled his foot. 'Aw. It ... it's all right. Fun'ral's not till Thursday.' He turned away abruptly to get on with his work.

She closed the door quietly.

'Who's that?' Kim came into the kitchen. 'Did I hear

27

voices?' She sounded bright, not about to offer any explanation for staying out until late again last night.

'The painter.' Raine thought an apology was due. But she wouldn't give Kim any excuse to become aggressive. 'I'm making coffee. What would you like to eat?'

'I never eat breakfast.'

'Do have something.'

'I don't want to get fat.'

'Some toast.'

'Okay,' Kim sighed, as if doing Raine a favour. She looked towards the window. Ginger's white-trousered legs were visible up on his ladder. 'Is that fella nice?'

Raine shrugged. 'He's a good worker.' So that's why Kim was down early; done up, complete with jade earrings. And wearing a green cotton granny skirt that made her look thinner than ever.

'Gonna give him coffee?'

'Later, probably. He's only just arrived.'

The prospect of his coming in to coffee, seemed to keep Kim happy. She hung around the foot of his ladder and, from time to time, called out, 'Hi!' Eventually she came in disgruntled. 'He dumb or something?'

'He can't hear when he's using his blowlamp.' Raine knew he would come down when he was ready. She put his usual mug on the side, and hoped Kim wasn't going to make herself a nuisance.

'Let me pour it for him,' Kim said later, after Raine had caught his eye, and he was on his way.

He declined to sit down but, as usual, leaned against the kitchen work-top. Kim made a great thing of pouring coffee, stopping when the mug was half full to roll her eyes and smile, 'Lots of milk, or more black?'

'Aw.' It seemed he couldn't find words.

'Fill it, Kim. Just a little milk.' Raine wished Kim would stop posturing.

Ginger watched Raine as she moved gracefully around the room, from table to fridge.

Kim asked, 'What's your name, do you like discos?'

28

'Aw.' He stopped.

She rolled her eyes and put her fair head on one side. 'Have you got a girlfriend?'

He went pink, his gold freckles stood out. 'Aw.' He hesitated. Moments later, he said, 'No.'

'No you don't like discos, or no you haven't got a girl-friend?'

'Let Ginger drink his coffee,' Raine tried to spare him. And herself.

'Oh, so it's Ginger, is it? Ginger for pluck.'

He avoided her flirting, almond eyes; he studied the red-tiled floor while he finished his drink.

When he had gone and it seemed he would be up the ladder for the rest of the morning, Kim announced she was going to Draymouth.

Raine's heart sank. But at least she knew this time where Kim was going. 'Must you stay out quite so late again, Kim?'

'School holidays, isn't it? Saw that whacky guy, I did. Might see him again.'

'Have you got enough money?' That whacky guy, as Kim called him, struck no alarm bells. If there had been any-thing doing, Kim would have been eager to report. Raine was more concerned with Kim's health.

'Will you get something to eat?'

'I'll have some Coke.'

'I said eat, Kim. You never eat. I'm sure your father will make you eat when he comes.'

'Don't want to get a great fat pig.'

'Perhaps,' Raine said, as if it would be something to look forward to, 'he'll take us out to a nice meal.'

'Then I'll stick my fingers down my throat and bring it up.'

Raine said no more, and watched her go; anything for a quiet life. Later, she saw that Ginger was busy burning off paint from an upper window sill, and knew she could trust him to be left. She wanted some fresh eggs and had noticed there was a farm about half a mile away that sold them.

She drove down the lane until she saw EGGS written in white chalk on a large blackboard stuck in the hedge.

She turned into the pitted farmyard. As she got out, a black and white collie bounded to her side. It nuzzled its head against her hand and, with closed eyes, enjoyed her spontaneous stroking, reassured this was a friend. An older dog, stretched on uneven cobbles, eyed her without lifting its head.

She looked about. Strewn implements, mounds of manure, discarded trailers, rusty iron. Numerous cats sniffed around the walls and between the bulging plastic sacks propped against them.

The farmhouse door stood open; she crossed and knocked on it with her knuckles. The dog followed. She knocked again, then peered round into a cluttered room; dark, with its low ceiling, small window, and jungle of pot plants. No one seemed to be in.

The dog pressed to her side, looked up at her, questioning. She smoothed its soft head, and looked back into the yard; outbuildings, old wooden feeding troughs, museum-like tools; a double-barrelled gun propped against a wall.

She sauntered around, took a handkerchief from her bag, wrinkled her nose at the pungent smell of ammonia, animal urine, and rotting silage.

Suddenly something caught her eye; she thought something moved between the slats of an old black shed. Closer, she peered through into the darkness. It moved again; pinkish brown with a tinge of blue; wet nostrils pushing against the slats as if trying to break through. Gradually she saw it was a calf, with scarcely room to move, standing knee-deep in its own muck.

She felt suddenly angry; with a violent urge to wrench open the creosoted slats, hear them splinter and break, and let the incarcerated animal out into the fresh air, probably to blink bewildered in the light. But free. FREE!

She heard something, and turned. A woman in a long brown dress disappeared into the house like a rat into a hole. From around the corner of the shed, a short, thick-set man appeared. He pointed at her with a double-barrelled gun.

Raine stood stock still as he approached. She didn't like his leer, but she wasn't afraid, she had done nothing wrong. He was probably just what he looked; a red-faced bully, about forty, with a greasy mat of black curly hair.

The dog, as if sensitive to some kind of ultrasonic vibrations that commanded subservience, slunk away from her side and sat down in the shadow of an old cart, watching.

"Afternoon, Miss. And what be you snoopin' round in yer for?'

She was already filled with a prejudice that his grubby open-neck check shirt did nothing to diminish; it strained over his beer gut which, in turn, ballooned offensively over the top of his trousers.

She moved towards the car. 'I came for some eggs, but I've changed my mind.' She took a handkerchief hurriedly from her bag and wiped her hands; she felt grubby already.

"Ow come?' His smile was stiff, as if not used often. 'Us 'ave got plenty.'

'I've changed my mind,' she repeated. She had heard about intensively fed animals, but had never seen.

He smirked and lowered his gun. 'I've seed this car go by yer oft times before, just lately 'ave'n I?'

She had guessed he only wanted to frighten her; to show his importance, prove who was Lord here. Now he wanted to be thought intelligent; he knew a stranger when he saw one.

'Probably. I've been here three weeks.' She got into her car, she felt more protected behind the wheel. She wound down the window and inclined her head towards the shed. 'I think it's cruel to keep animals like that, it shouldn't be allowed.'

He glared; his face turned puce. 'Who asked your bloody 'pinion?'

She switched on the engine and engaged reverse.

31

He shouted, 'You don't know nought about it, you bloody don't. 'Oo asked you to come snoopin' round?'

She revved to back from the bumpy yard, partly drowning his parting invective that rose louder and louder to follow her out.

'Bloody interfering young bitch. I'll set the dogs on you next time, I bloody will, see if I don't.'

She felt shaken and nearly collided with another car turning into the yard. It was wrong, animals kept like that. But what good had she done? Probably sounded stupid, spoken out of turn and got herself disliked.

At least she need never encounter that revolting man again. She wouldn't buy his eggs if she were starving. Come to think of it, she hadn't seen any chickens in that disgusting yard; they, too, were probably imprisoned somewhere in a deep-litter shed or, worse still, in those battery cages that she hated to think of.

She put him out of her mind. The sun was warm again. The lasting dry spell was gradually turning the long grasses to shades of brown and orange, encouraging them to seed.

She drove up to the common and parked in a clearing under the trees. Other cars, parked nearby, were mostly empty while their owners walked away along the narrow pathways through the scrub.

Usually, the wide open space made her feel at peace. Today, from her car, she looked out, unseeing. Deep inside her was a dull ache; she had known it ever since Kim's arrival, and it took the edge from everything that had been so wonderful before.

She tried to smother the feeling but, instead of going away, it was building up. She had kept her cool in spite of everything that had nearly driven her crazy in the past few days, because Kim was Jeff's own flesh and blood. And where had it got her? Softly softly was a slow game. At moments, she was frightened. She didn't want to play it any more. She supposed she would have to go on trying, just a little longer.

* * *

When she arrived home, Ginger was packing his van. He looked towards her with one of his nervous smiles that seemed to indicate that he had something to say.

She went over. 'How are things going?'

'Aw.' He cleared his throat. 'Sh ... she ... the girl come back.' He hesitated. 'She's gone again.'

'Thanks. I don't suppose you know where, this time?'

'Sh ... she w ... wanted me to ... to take her for ... for a ride.'

'Where, for heaven's sake?'

'J ... just a ride.' He looked deep into Raine's eyes. 'Do sh ... she upset you?'

'She is a bit of a responsibility. Thank goodness her father is coming back here on Wednesday. Tomorrow night.'

'I ... I didn't look.' Ginger shook his head from side to side, his eyes closed. 'I swear ... I swear I didn't see.'

'What do you mean?'

'Aw. The girl. Sh ... she were cross ... ww ... when I said I wouldn't ... wouldn't take her.' His pale eyes drilled into Raine as if he willed her to believe him. 'Sh ... she went in then ... I ... I think sh ... she changed her dress. I didn't see, God's honour I never. I come down the ladder.'

'Are you trying to tell me she accused you of looking in the bedroom window?'

'I never. I come down. God's honour.'

'Oh I believe you, Ginger, don't worry. I'm just so terribly sorry about this, I really am.' She saw his anxiety, the gold eyelashes, and pallid cheeks. 'I could murder her, I really could. Behaving so badly.' She paused to collect herself, as much ashamed of giving vent to her own true feelings as of Kim's misconduct. 'I mean ... just when you're so upset with your own troubles. It's unforgivable.'

He adjusted his extending ladder to lie alongside a short one on the roof of his van. 'Aw. I ... I'm glad you believe me. Sh ... she upsets you, too, don't she?'

'I try to make friends.' She didn't want to discuss Kim further, and moved to go.

His voice surprised her and she turned to face him. She had thought him incapable of sounding positive about anything, let alone angry.

He said: 'I ... I ... I don't like it! I mean ... to think she upsets you!'

The look in his eyes embarrassed her. 'Oh, don't worry about me. Do we see you tomorrow, okay?'

'Aw. Yes. Not Thursday.'

Indoors, she went upstairs. Her room was on the side of the house that overlooked the common; the side where Ginger had been working. She was never sure whether you would call it the front, or the back of the house.

Kim's room was on the other side, overlooking the lane with its overgrown summer hedges, and the big iron gates at the entrance to the short drive that were usually kept open, except at night.

If Kim had tried to flaunt herself while changing her clothes, to attract Ginger's attention, she couldn't have been in her own room.

Perhaps she had merely looked out from Raine's window, and pretended she thought Ginger had seen her changing, just to tease him; make an issue. It was the sort of thing she would do.

Raine straightened Jeffrey's photo on the dressing table, and the one of her beloved parents next to it, that was out of line, too. Kim *had* been here, mucking around, and had obviously used her make-up. Raine returned her lip-brush and eye-shadow to their proper places.

The curtains had been disturbed. She straightened them, arranged their neat folds, then fetched a pan and brush; it was inevitable that some dust and small flakes of paint would have drifted in from outside, she had allowed for that.

A little later, she realised it was going to be another evening of waiting for Kim to come in. She didn't worry as much as before; Kim would turn up in her own good time, making school holidays a good excuse.

But she hoped Jeffrey wouldn't ring as late as he had last

night when she had lied, said Kim was in bed, because she thought that was what he would want to hear.

She was a bit thrown when he had sounded very surprised, but she could hardly go back on her word. And had she imagined a certain animosity against Kim that she had never heard before? Had he been tired? Frustrated because he hadn't succeeded yet in finding her a suitable boarding school?

She felt it unlike him to say the things he had. She had thought him a fond father, and had been impressed by his parental firmness, shown with chivalry on Kim's first evening here. Had he been more angry with Kim then, than he had allowed himself to show? Was it an act, a restrained resoluteness shown to impress her, more than Kim?

Last night, on the phone, she had found herself actually taking Kim's side; just a little, to play things down; she didn't like hearing Jeffrey so angry. Instead, she must have said the wrong thing and had, unwittingly, added strength to his unexpected rancour.

He had said angrily that if Kim threatened to spoil things between them, he would murder the little minx! No one, and nothing, was going to stop them from being happy in their new environment.

Now she tried to read while she waited for Kim to come home. But she couldn't concentrate. It had been dark for nearly two hours, and when she heard a car stop outside, her hopes rose.

Moments later, Kim burst in. She sounded pleased. 'I had a taxi. You did say to.'

'Oh good. Yes. Of course. I'm glad you did.' So Ginger was right, Raine saw. Kim had changed. In contrast to this morning's long granny dress, her leather skirt barely showed beneath the man's jacket she was wearing, sleeves pushed to her elbows.

'And I've seen that whacky guy again. William.' She peeled off the jacket and dropped it on the floor.

'Who?'

'William. His name's William. You know.'

'Do I?'

'Yes. You know. Him with the hymn books.'

'Oh him. He doesn't like girls.'

'Big deal.'

'Where did he take you?'

'Didn't take me anywhere. Saw him. Near the church.'

Raine looked pointedly at the jacket on the drawing-room carpet. 'Be earlier tomorrow. Your father's coming.'

'Seeing William.' Reluctantly she picked up the jacket, threw it like a cape around her shoulders and slumped into an armchair.

'He's asked you?'

'I know where he'll be.'

'Hardly the same thing. Have you talked?'

'' Course, what do you think?' Kim stretched out her long skinny legs. 'I made him. He's brill. D'you know, his eyes are little windows. Casements. Like in houses.'

Intrigued, Raine scarcely noticed the huge canvas hold-all join the jacket on the carpet, as Kim prattled on. 'When the windows are open, his soul comes out.'

Raine wondered if she was meant to be amused. 'Sounds like a weather vane to me.'

'No. True. Listen. It goes all round people. His soul. Protects them. Helps them from sin.'

'Whatever makes you think that?' Raine had heard of Billy Graham. And instant conversions. But *this*.

'He said so. So I asked to look. You know. Right into his eyes. Close. To see his soul.'

'Did you?'

'Why not?'

'See his soul, I mean.'

'Don't know. Think that's when I kissed him.'

'You what?'

'Oh, don't you sound like a convent teacher?' Kim slipped off her shoes.

Raine reached over to a small table and put down the book she hadn't been able to read. Relieved now that Kim was in, she felt ready for bed.

Kim stretched again. 'He went all queer. Twitching. Shaky. He began breathing ever so hard; panting, like he'd been jogging for miles.' She looked amused and kicked her shoes across the room. 'He's never kissed a girl before. He began to cry. Said God was looking.' She laughed. 'He said he had sinned.'

'Kim. You shouldn't. You really must be careful.' Raine tried not to sound the heavy old aunt and thought it best to change the subject for the time being, and let Jeffrey deal with Kim when he came. 'Now, won't you have a hot drink before you go to bed?'

'It's fun. Seeing how boys go. All breathless and moaning. Barry always went like that.'

'Who's Barry?'

'One of Monica's boyfriends.'

'You mean your mother's?'

'Big deal. Monica's.'

'But her boyfriend?'

'Most of them liked me best. When she wasn't around.' Kim ran her fingers through her bubbly hair to puff it out. 'All except John. He didn't. Not her precious John.'

Raine wasn't interested. Kim liked to boast. 'I asked you, would you like a hot drink?'

'I've had a Coke,' Kim said not willing to be put off her train of reminiscence. 'Precious John thought he was going to marry Monica.'

Raine discerned Kim's loose, confessional mood, as if she might have been drinking something stronger than Coke. 'What happened?'

'I told her he had tried to come it with me. You know. Some funny business. Like they do.'

'Kim! How awful. The bastard!'

'He wouldn't. Like the others did. He was crazy about *her.*'

'You mean you lied to your mother?'

'He shouldn't have called me a silly little girl when I was being nice to him. So I got my own back.'

'But your mother; what you told her wasn't true.'

Kim laughed. 'She chucked him, anyway. Served him right.' Kim laughed again as if it was a huge joke. 'He nearly went mad. He tried to frighten me. He put his hands around my neck and vowed he would get me one day.'

5

Raine tried not to let Kim's disclosures keep her awake, which wasn't difficult with the comforting thought that Jeffrey would be here tomorrow. She hadn't wanted to burden him, on the phone, with what might sound like two petty women unable to get on together.

Perhaps Kim would be different with his authority around and, if not, well, he would be able to see for himself how intolerable things were.

In that more positive frame of mind she fell asleep and, after a good night, woke up extra early on Wednesday morning.

Her subconscious mind had reminded her that today she had something to look forward to, and also that she wanted to wash and dress and be out of her bedroom before Ginger arrived to resume working on the upper windows.

She was downstairs, preparing her breakfast grapefruit, when she heard him arrive; the van door slammed. He usually wasted no time before sliding his ladders from the roof-rack and getting on with his work; so she was surprised, moments later, to hear his gentle tap on the back door.

'Good morning,' she greeted him, noting his pale face and the smell of paint he always brought.

'Aw.' He hesitated, as if he hadn't prepared himself for her opening the door so promptly. 'You ... you're all right then?'

'Yes thanks.' She was unprepared for his solicitude. 'Shouldn't I be?'

'Aw. Aw yes.' He paused again. 'She come home then?'

'Y ... e ... s,' she said slowly, her voice questioning. She assumed of course he meant Kim.

39

'Aw. Th ... that's all right then. Long as she got back. I wondered ... if you was all right ... were worried like.'

'I'm fine, thanks,' she smiled, trying not to let him see he had perturbed her, but at the same time wanting to catch what he muttered as he turned away; something about young girls round the docks ... their business.

She closed the door, her smile gone; kind of him to be concerned, but the need was humiliating; it had spoilt the start of her new day.

At least the day promised, weather-wise, to be another grand one; only a few puffy white clouds, like sublimated sheep, in the high blue sky.

She usually had breakfast in the kitchen if she was alone. When Kim appeared, wearing green tights and court shoes that mis-matched her crumpled eau-de-nil skirt, she thought, not unkindly, that the girl's complete lack of dress sense made her look like a sapling that wasn't going to make it. 'Coffee?'

Kim sat down. Without a word she drank thirstily and pushed her cup forward for a refill. After a third cup, drunk in sullen silence, Raine thought she detected signs of dehydration.

'Will you have some toast?'

'I never eat breakfast.'

'A grapefruit wouldn't make you fat.'

'I've told you. How many more times?'

Raine resented the undeserved hostility; felt she might as well counter it now; show a modicum of authority. 'Kim,' she said, her voice firm but gently modulated. 'You know, you ought not to go near the docks in Draymouth ... the public houses ... I believe they can get rough there.'

Kim looked at her over the rim of her cup.

Raine was aware that the almond-shaped eyes were half closed, like a cat blinking into the sun. 'You're under age, you'll get landlords into trouble, besides yourself.'

'Big deal. Go if I want.'

'Your father will be here tonight.'

'Big deal.'

40

Determined to seem casual, not to labour the issue, Raine got up, taking some plates to the sink. 'If you've finished, I can wash up.'

'It would be a pity to leave the things for five minutes,' Kim said, elbows on the table. 'They might get stained.' She pushed her saucer forward with her arm; her cup fell onto its side with a rattle.

Raine ignored the childish outburst. She pushed the brightly patterned cotton curtains clear of the draining board.

'You're so fussy, a real fusspot,' Kim hissed.

Raine ignored her.

'You've touched those curtains three times already since I've been here.'

'They were blowing in over the tap,' Raine said levelly. 'I'm not fussy.'

'Oh no? Big deal.' Kim rested her face in her cupped hands, and narrowed her eyes. 'You are fussy. You're so fussy I bet you put your nightdress on a hanger.'

'Oh, don't try to be silly.'

'You're always straightening things ... putting chairs straight ... making pictures stand in line.'

Raine felt her cheeks grow hot. Thank goodness Jeff would soon be here. She tidied the draining board for something to do; Kim might shut up if she got little response.

'I bet those side-on Christmas cards must drive you crazy ... you know ... the sort that won't stand up straight.' Kim paused. '*They* won't stand in line. You're daft. Don't know what Jeff ... er ... ee sees in you.' She looked round the kitchen with its expensive new fittings. 'Money I suppose. That's what. Heard Monica say you're not hard up for a quid or two.'

Raine's blood boiled; of all the nasty, insolent offspring. Could this really be Jeffrey's flesh and blood? 'Well, if you're going to be quarrelsome...'

'Well then,' Kim snapped, 'who's been telling tales about me, then?' She paused. 'That creep out there I bet.' She

41

shouted: 'He's daft! Aw aw aw, all he can say is aw aw, he's just like a donkey!'

Her voice rose to an angry shriek, 'And don't think I haven't seen the way he looks at you. Up and down. Like he's seeing you naked. I bet he screws you when I'm not here.'

Raine swung round from the sink. 'How dare you! How dare you, Kim! Apologise at once!'

The girl looked only momentarily sheepish, then attempted to justify herself. 'You let Jeff ... er ... ee, so why not that aw aw donkey?' Bolder she shouted: 'I know he screws you.'

Raine suddenly realised the window was wide open, she turned and hastily pulled the bottom half shut behind the sink. 'How dare you! How dare you!' she repeated, keeping her voice down as she confronted Kim again.

Her heart raced. She was unused to coarseness; vulgarity was no part of her upbringing, nor of her years spent as a private secretary to a titled landowner. She was completely lost for words, except, 'Apologise at once.'

'Why should I? Think I don't know he screws you?'

Raine's hand raised involuntarily. She stopped it in mid-air as what she was about to do flashed through her mind; and she had never hit anyone in her life.

She felt as if her whole being burned. In that blinding moment of provocation, she had been about not only to slap Kim's face, she had wanted just as fiercely to put her hands around that little white throat until Kim took back every word. As long as those young vocal cords could utter sound, they were going to make trouble.

Raine was restrained by a lifetime of genteel upbringing. She stood rigid, looking down at the small, unrepentant face.

Kim said, 'Monica's the same. Called them my uncles. Till I found out uncles don't go to bed with your mother.' She smiled, and added as if claiming victory, 'Then she used to send me to the pictures. Big deal. So I saw all the latest films.' She got up.

42

'You're not leaving this kitchen until you've apologised.'

'Big deal. Going out.'

'Your father's coming...'

'Be back by then. Tell him my side,' she shouted, turning.

'You'll apologise first.' Raine grabbed her shoulders, bunching the thin cotton dress in her hands; it was like trying to handle a strong eel.

'Let go, you silly cow!' Kim screamed, twisting to wrench free. 'Let go of me, silly cow,' her voice rose hysterically. 'Let go ... o ... ooo!'

Suddenly she stopped screaming and grasped Raine's hands in her own; she pushed them slightly away then up to her mouth and bit deep into Raine's arm above the wrist with teeth as sharp as broken glass.

Raine writhed; even in her agony, aware of Ginger outside, she suppressed crying out.

Kim stopped biting and, without a glance at the blood that splattered down Raine's dress and onto the polished tiled floor, she dashed to the door. 'Who's sorry now, then? Aw aw donkey. Aw aw.'

Raine turned on the cold tap. The water stung as it washed over the red weal and broken skin, and mixed with the blood that poured from her arm and down over her hand. She held a clean dry towel over it to staunch the flow while she found a suitable dressing in her kitchen first-aid kit.

She slumped down in her chair at the table and buried her face in her hands. She wanted to cry but the tears wouldn't come, she felt all twisted inside. Sick.

She pressed her hands over her ears to lesson the sound of the Sony upstairs which, turned up to full blast, she felt sure could be heard in Draymouth. She prayed, please Jeffrey, please come quickly, spare me any more of this.

But first there was the whole day to get through. And if she didn't make coffee for Ginger as she had done for the past two and a half weeks, he would think something was wrong, if he didn't already.

When coffee time came, she avoided his eyes; but it was difficult pretending to be busy when you felt like doing nothing, and actually had little to do. She guessed Ginger saw through her constant opening and shutting of the smart built-in cupboards, her trips to and from the fridge, her apparent studious perusal of her cookery book.

'Aw,' he opened up suddenly, 'Sh ... she upsets you, don't she? G ... g ... got a temper, has she?'

'No. No ... just teenage...' Raine said lightly, and as if surprised by his remark; but she felt humiliated; she didn't want to discuss Kim; why should she explain things to him?

'Sh ... she do. I ... I won't have ... I don't like her to upset you.'

Raine felt her colour rise. God! The way he looked at her, as if searching her mind, if not her body. She looked away. 'Oh, don't worry, she doesn't worry me.' She picked up her cookery book again and leafed through the pages.

She wished he would hurry up and go; this was degrading; what exactly had he heard? The kitchen window had been wide open at the top, it was too high for her to shut quickly without getting on a chair, so she had left it.

She could understand why he obviously disliked Kim, she had accused him of being a peeping Tom. Did her silly behaviour also account for the glacial steel in his eyes, and the cut in his voice when he spoke of her?

She measured out the rest of the day, just one hour at a time. There was no meal to prepare. Jeffrey was going to be late and, to save her, he was having something on the way. Kim had made it quite clear that she was hell-bent on starving to death, though she made an occasional sulky appearance to help herself to a dry biscuit, and a drink of orange.

By four o'clock Raine tired of going round the house, arranging flowers, touching things, twitching curtains, and realigning photographs of Jeffrey, and her beloved lost parents, and funny Aunt Jo.

She made some tea; and took it into the garden. It was shady on the east side of the house; the air was less heavy with bees and she watched a family of sparrows, flicking and writhing, small wings outstretched as they enjoyed a dust-bath in the flower bed of spent roses.

At half past four she heard Ginger slam the door of his van and drive off. She checked her watch. He had gone early. Perhaps he had a lot to do, his mother's funeral tomorrow.

But he hadn't looked around the corner of the house to say 'cheerio' as he usually did. God! She wondered, what exactly had he heard this morning? Kim's raised voice, those disgusting accusations, the dreadful words she used? Had she herself retaliated too loudly? They must have sounded like a couple of fishwives.

At least everything was quiet now. No blaring, continuous pop on that confounded Sony. No gentle sounds of Ginger removing old paint. Even the birds seemed not to sing in August.

She whittled the long evening away; had a shower; a manicure; washed and dried her hair, and set it back from her face with a fresh band of brown ribbon.

She watched the setting sun light the common. As it sank to the top of a far hill, it sent a metallic path across the wide river that bounded Draymouth on the west. This area, renowned for its sunsets according to the guidebooks, had inspired the likes of Turner and Danby. Perhaps here, with such copy, she would be able to improve on her own early efforts that hung in the dining room above the fireplace.

The distant sea and the flinty pathways glinted over the common. Parked cars, windscreens, her own west-facing windows had become blinding blobs of blood orange. When the last fiery arc dropped behind the hill, it was as if some gigantic lighted chandelier had been switched off, leaving the residual glow and the darkening sky seared with streaks of red, bruise-purple, and gold.

She settled with a book in the drawing room, but couldn't concentrate to read. What exactly could she tell Jeff about Kim?

It grew darker and she switched on more lights. The

scent of flowers came through the open window as she waited impatiently, and time dragged.

At last she heard a car, but it seemed to have stopped outside in the lane, then its door slammed and it was driven on. Moments later the door bell chimed.

She started. Of course, the man had come to collect her car, she had momentarily forgotten. But she had everything ready for him, she reflected, as she went to the door. The documents only needed signing; there was plenty of light over the garage and in the porch, she wouldn't need to ask him in, and he wouldn't know that she was here on her own.

She recognised the swarthy complexion, and the villainous-looking tattoos on the man's arms beneath his short-sleeved shirt, as he counted out the balance he owed her from bundles of grubby twenty-pound notes.

Wasting little time, he backed her red Ford from the garage, out through the drive, turned the wheel and sped down the lane.

What a time to come, she thought. And no apology. We might have been in bed asleep for all he knew. But she and Jeff weren't in bed, and she wondered where, exactly, was he? He had said he would be here latish, but she hadn't reckoned on his being this late.

It seemed only moments later that she heard him. He might almost have been in time to see her own car being driven away, could even have had to pull into one of the bays for it to pass.

He came into the drawing room. Without a word he sat down heavily into an armchair opposite her, rested his head back against a cushion and shut his eyes.

'What's up, Jeff?'

'There was an accident.'

'Oh no, Jeff! Not you ... you all right?' She knew every inch of the square, downright face, the well-shaped dark brows and smooth firm chin, but had never seen his broad forehead so furrowed.

He got up and poured himself a whisky from a bottle on

46

the small side table. He tipped it back, poured another, and sat down.

She watched as he rested the small cut-glass tumbler on the palm of one hand while the long well-manicured fingers of the other circled and tapped it lightly as if he were playing a musical instrument.

She guessed he needed time to compose himself after whatever had happened. This was not the moment to tell him that Kim wasn't here. He hadn't asked; neither had he kissed her; nor answered her question.

'Was it a car? Were you involved?' She was afraid to ask more; the subject was almost taboo, and with a tense gathering of fine lines around his dark eyes, he looked very tired. But she had to know. 'Was anyone hurt ... or...?' She couldn't bring herself to say killed.

He didn't answer right away. When he did, it was as if he was having to think back, hard. 'I ... I don't know. Didn't see.' He sipped his drink. 'There was a car stopped in front of me. I reversed. Took a side road.'

In those circumstances, it seemed to Raine that he had no need to be quite so affected. She tried to understand; make allowance. She had never got over his past experience. She waited until he seemed more relaxed after another drink, before she mentioned her own worry. 'Jeff ... Kim's not here.'

'Kim?' He started. 'Sorry. I hadn't asked, what with everything.' He hesitated. 'So she's gone back to Monica, already?'

'No. She's ... not in.'

'The little devil. Nearly half past ten. Where's she gone, what time did she go?'

'I don't know.' Raine knew it sounded feeble, but the account she had been rehearsing had gone. 'I ... I thought she was in her room,' she added, steeling herself for a tirade of paternal anxiety. Instead, she detected the same hint of animosity towards Kim that she had imagined when he spoke on the phone.

'It's not the first time, is it? Out late, I mean?' He

47

finished his whisky. 'I guessed she was playing you up when I rang. You didn't have to tell me.' He put his glass on the small table at his side. 'And I've been determined not to let her come between me and you.'

He held out his arms. 'Come on, darling, onto my lap. D'you realise I haven't even kissed you yet.'

She warmed to him, at the same time surprised by his unconcern. She had been keyed up, prepared for his inevitable deep anxiety, his possible recriminations. Filled with guilt she had the gut feeling that whatever his reaction, he might blame her.

Briefly she enjoyed his lips on hers. She tried not to disappoint him, and to respond with equal ardour to his hungry kisses. But even his caresses, the tingling touch of his hand smoothing her breasts, failed to arouse her. The creeping weed of guilt was already spoiling everything.

A sound outside, made them start. A rustle of shrubs under the open window; possible light steps on the gravel. Raine sat back on her own chair, afraid, yet relieved; she hadn't felt like making love, and wouldn't have to go on pretending.

They looked at each other.

'Has she a key?' Jeffrey asked.

'No. She comes in the back. It's open.'

Soon they realised that any footsteps they might have imagined had gone away. More moments passed. Kim didn't come in. Jeffrey got up.

Raine watched him lean out of the window before he turned and strode purposefully across the room. Irrelevantly she noted that the cut of his light grey trousers still looked good after his long journey, but the back of his blue cotton shirt was badly creased.

She heard him hurry out, leaving the front door open. She waited, heart in mouth. She was afraid when he came back alone, his anxiety might turn to anger, and she would have to endure the accusations which her guilt made her sure were bound to come.

He seemed a long time gone. The brass carriage clock,

glass-domed on the side table, seemed to have barely moved its hands since the last time she looked.

When at last he came in, she began, 'What...?'

'Not a sign ... do you get many cars by here?'

'Not a lot. But some occasionally. I think they're probably with couples going home from up on the common.'

He said: 'I was just in time to see some tail lights disappearing round the bend down the lane.' He sat down heavily and stretched his long legs. 'I didn't hear anything, the engine must have been switched off. Very considerate, some people.'

'You were a long time.'

'I wasn't.'

'It seemed a long time.'

'Well, I did go up and down a bit. Naturally. And I climbed up the bank and peered over the hedge.' He paused, and smiled. 'Going to come on my lap again?'

She hadn't expected him to sound so unconcerned, after all her trepidation. She shook her head.

He shrugged. 'Oh well, if that's how you feel. I thought perhaps ... just a cuddle ... while we wait.'

Their eyes met; his held the look that usually weakened her knees and set her body alight beneath her clothes. Now she felt in no mood to be cuddled.

Jeffrey poured himself another whisky, and they sat a long while without speaking until he said: 'Do you think we should inform the police, Raine?'

She hesitated. 'Perhaps we should.'

'I suppose we could wait a bit longer,' he said. 'She's been very late before.'

Later, Raine said: 'Jeff ... don't you think ... perhaps now...?'

He set his tumbler down. 'Maybe ... but we don't want to look fools if she turns up in the meantime, do we?'

They waited; each locked in their separate silences. Each reacted to every murmur among the trees; in the bushes nearby, or to the movement of the front door that Jeffrey hadn't closed properly, and to the occasional imagined

49

click of the so-called back door which was actually on the side of the drive that led into the kitchen.

Over two hours passed. Reluctantly they agreed that it was growing more likely that, either by the front or the back door, Kim was not going to come in.

6

Raine was never quite sure which of them eventually agreed to act and phone Draymouth Police Station.

It was 2.30 a.m. that Detective Sergeant Roger Mills logged his arrival. Even without the starry sky and a sliver of moon, the isolated house had been easy to find. Lights shone from every window, and an impressive carriage-lamp blazed from the creeper-covered wall by the open front door.

The DS was a bright-eyed, wiry but slightly-built man in his early thirties. What he lacked in girth he made up for in ambition having, after two years on the beat, applied to join the CID determined to get on.

He sat in Raine's tastefully furnished drawing room, and listened to a case that sounded to be no more than that of a rebellious young stop-out, but none the less worrying for Miss Barclay and the girl's father.

He had always found, when dealing with missing persons, that it helped him psychologically if he could see something of the surroundings they had left behind. It often proved of practical value, too; a place, or a room, could be left so full of a person, it could tell a lot.

Raine flinched when he made a polite request to look all around the house. To be told that he would especially like to see Kim's room, was as if she had been asked to strip naked in public.

It sparked childhood memories of living with Aunt Jo after her parents were killed. You could never find anything you wanted, the book you had put down, a matching pair of clean socks for school, or the jigsaw you'd started. Everything always got covered with clutter. She had vowed

51

then, that when she had a house of her own, it would be clean, tidy, and organised. Now she had to let an outsider, a complete stranger, see Kim's room.

The crumpled, lumpy camp bed had obviously been lounged on since the morning when Kim had skimpily pulled over the covers; possessions filled the hollows, and the pink-flowered bedspread trailed on the floor.

Beneath the temporary, make-do chair and table, were teenage magazines, slithered from the piles above. Split cardboard boxes spilled cassettes over the floor to join little piles of abandoned clothes; the crumpled green cotton granny skirt, a man's check jacket, and tiny pink knickers with lace hearts near the crotch.

Worst of all, Raine hated the posters. Crude colours, simulated splashes of blood, life-size gyrating rock stars, bizarre figures and white-painted cadaverous faces with empty eye sockets.

They had been the last straw. Wretched posters; some with corners already parted from their sticky tape and keeling over like autumn leaves about to fall.

She suspected, had there been cupboards to look into, or beds to look under, the Detective Sergeant would have done so. He surveyed what there was; the beautifully clean ceiling, fresh paintwork, bright, pretty flower-patterned curtains, and what was left still visible of the good green carpet.

'What a nice pleasant room,' he said, turning to indicate he had seen enough.

Raine felt her face colour. How could he! What must he really be thinking; that she was a slut?

He looked round her own room; in the bathroom, and the big cupboard on the landing, before he turned to go downstairs. She led the way, thankful that was over. Now he could go.

Contrary to her hope, he produced a large torch; he wanted to search the garden, the garage, had they a shed? She was surprised, when he had finished, that he came into the drawing room again, sat down, notebook in hand and, as if he hadn't asked enough questions already, started again:

'Now, can you tell me exactly what the girl was wearing?'

Raine felt her burden of responsibility the heavier because Jeffrey wasn't expected to know. He was lucky. Not having been here, he could stay silent.

'She was wearing a black leather miniskirt. I think.'

'You're not sure?'

'I ... I didn't actually see her go.'

'Did you notice if it was still upstairs?'

She had been too conscious of the messy room to notice anything specific, and what did it matter? 'No. I didn't notice. I mean ... I'm sure it wasn't.'

'We can check again directly. What else was she wearing?'

Raine bit her thumb, thinking, before she remembered. 'Green tights ... well she had green tights on in the morning.'

'And you didn't actually see her go out in them?'

'Well ... no.'

He shifted his big feet. With pen poised over his notebook he said: 'Well, tell me what you saw her wearing the last time you saw her dressed ... you say ... in the morning.'

Raine slowly recalled: 'Black miniskirt ... leather. Green tights ... oh, and a T-shirt.'

'What colour?'

'Er ... orange ... yes, definitely orange.'

'Anything special about it? Any picture like they have, or a logo?'

Raine linked her hands and squeezed her fingers. How much did she have to tell, was it all necessary? 'There were some letters.'

'Letters?'

'Well ... words.'

'What were they?'

Raine didn't answer.

Mills prompted her. 'You remember that the T-shirt was definitely orange. Can't you remember the words?'

'Well ... yes ... on the front it said ... "I am a virgin".'
She saw he didn't bat an eyelid.

He went on writing. 'And? I notice you said "on the front". Was there anything on the back?'

She considered a moment. There was a time when she might have smiled at the thought, but nothing was funny any more. 'Well ... there was ... something like...' She paused, then added quickly, '"But this is a very old T-shirt".'

He finished putting it down. 'Was she carrying anything; like a handbag?'

'A large yellow shoulder bag.'

'Like the yellow holdall up in her room?'

'Is it? Was it?' Raine hadn't noticed.

'Perhaps she's got more than one. Has she?'

'No, no, I don't think so.' Raine blushed. His casual perfunctory glance upstairs had been deceiving, obviously he hadn't missed a thing. 'If it's up there, she didn't take it. I didn't see it. I'm sorry.' She supposed it was natural he should give her a hard look. The bag was big enough.

'How tall is she?' he asked.

Raine looked at Jeffrey, over six foot.

He answered for her: 'About five foot nine. Very tall for her age.'

Raine elaborated: 'She looked taller because she was so thin.'

The sergeant glanced up from his book, his sharp eyes met Raine's. 'Looked? Was?'

Confused, not sure what he was getting at, she mumbled, 'Well...'

'Perhaps you meant "she looks taller, she is so thin"?'

She realised her mistake, and he had put words back in her mouth. 'Yes. Of course.'

'And her eyes? What colour are they?'

The questions went on. Her hair, what colour? Short or long, straight or curly? Does she wear make-up? Has she any distinguishing marks on her face, on her limbs, or on her body? Any moles or scars? Is she fair-skinned, or suntanned?

54

At last, it seemed, Detective Sergeant Mills had all he wanted to know; everything was under control. The duty officer at the Station had already alerted night patrols to be on the lookout. He had contacted Divisional Police Headquarters, and reported the girl missing. The Detective Chief Superintendent would be notified; he normally waited twenty-four hours and if the girl didn't turn up, her description would be issued, and appeals made on local radio.

What was left of the night dragged on into Thursday. Some time during the day, two cars arrived at the same time. The first wore a brand new registration number; the second car was to take the driver of the new car back to the garage.

Raine scarcely noticed. Beyond the fact that the new car was cream, a colour the glossy brochure ostentatiously described as champagne, and it was sparkling clean, she didn't care much.

The mechanic had put it in the garage for her and shut the door. After the months of eager waiting, she felt as though delivered of a child and, in the pain of the moment, not wanting to look at it.

There had been nothing really wrong with her old red Ford except a few scratches, but she hated things when they began to look tatty, and she could, after all, spend her own money as she wished.

She had such high hopes when she and Jeffrey bought this house. They had come down to the west country and spent a week looking at properties after he had been appointed manager of his firm's Draymouth office.

They were going to make a new life. They would get married and forget Jeff's past, now that his divorce was finalised, and Monica had custody of Kim. Or did have, Raine reflected bitterly, until Kim decided she would rather live with her father.

There was no forgetting the girl. Two plain clothes police officers called during the day. There were more questions. Endless questions. Had they a photograph of Kim? She hadn't. Her mother most certainly would have one, where did she live?

On Friday, the police issued Kim's description. Raine first heard it broadcast on the local radio, with an appeal for anyone who might have seen Kim to get in touch with Draymouth police.

After lunch, YOUNG GIRL MISSING was front page news in the local evening paper.

Raine felt isolated; vulnerable. Jeffrey had gone into the Draymouth office where he was due to start his new appointment on Monday. He hoped if possible to have the date deferred on compassionate grounds.

An Incident Room was being set up in the village hall, and house-to-house teams had been called.

Who in the village, she wondered, had seen Kim, and would remember? The exercise seemed pointless, no one knew her, she had been here just seven days and most of them she had spent in Draymouth. She pictured housewives down in the village being brought to their doorsteps and questioned by uniformed officers carrying clipboards. If she knew anything about country people, they in turn would try asking the policemen questions. If they didn't get answers, which they probably wouldn't, they would speculate and start to spread rumours.

She went round the house, touching things, moving them, putting them back as they were, straightening the curtains.

She was aware that Ginger had been outside all day. He obviously had been getting on with the painting, conscientiously, as if he were trying to make up for his not coming yesterday. She had heard the occasional drag of his ladder, his footsteps on the gravel, his van door slammed as he left to go home.

Why did she feel guilty because today she hadn't once offered him coffee? She had felt unable to even face him. She had left it to Jeffrey to go outside and introduce himself, to say a polite word or two. He hadn't stayed long;

Ginger, with his nervous 'Aws' took a long time to say little, and Jeffrey was inclined to be impatient.

She hadn't told Jeffrey about Ginger's coming in to coffee, or of his way of looking at her, his intensity when speaking of his concern that Kim upset her.

Nor had she told him of Ginger's afternoon encounter with Kim, the petulant accusations she had made when he wouldn't take her for a ride in his van. Petty tales out of school, like the other terrible things Kim had said, had nothing to do with the situation they were in.

Raine didn't want to speak of them to anyone; speaking only enlarged; and she wanted them to go away.

It was typical of Ginger not to have mentioned anything of the past few days to Jeffrey, either. Ginger was a man of very few words, unless drawn. He had probably returned Jeffrey's polite remarks, then looked at the clouds building up and said that he was anxious to get on with the painting before the weather broke.

She wondered if the police had got round yet to calling at his house. It would be known that he worked here, and that he must have seen Kim. Would he tell them what he knew; tell them of Kim's accusation that he was a peeping Tom, tell of hearing raised, angry voices?

Would he tell them with the same conviction and look of concern as when he told her, that the girl upset her? Raine could see his penetrating pale blue eyes now, looking into hers when he said: 'I don't like it. She upsets you.'

Spiritless, she looked in the fridge-freezer, and the kitchen wall-cupboards. They needed replenishing. Perhaps tomorrow Jeffrey would take her to do some shopping in Draymouth. If she went to the Post Office Stores in the village, although few people really knew her, she imagined there would be exchanged looks, and nudged elbows.

The phone rang, cutting through her thoughts; it could only be Jeff.

It was Drayford Incident Room. Detective Sergeant Roger Mills would like a few words with Mr Croft if he would please call in.

Raine promised to give Jeffrey the message. She sat down in the kitchen, next to the coffee pot; it was all she had seemed to do all day, drink coffee in the kitchen, unable to relax anywhere else. Now, she asked herself, tensed up again, why Drayford Incident Room? That was the third time Detective Mills had rung. And why Jeffrey?

She waited impatiently for him to come in. He was late, she had been expecting him any minute for the past hour. Perhaps traffic was heavy, Friday was market day. She sipped her coffee. The phone rang again. She put down her cup and went to answer it.

For a moment, it seemed there was no one there. No one answered her repeated 'Hellos' and 'Who is it?' She asked again: 'Who's calling?' She felt there was someone at the end of the line, perhaps they'd found they had the wrong number. 'Hello? This is Draymouth seven three two one.'

She was about to replace the receiver on its cradle when she heard a voice. She didn't recognise it, or what he was saying. She asked: 'What number were you wanting? This is seven three two one.'

There was a pause. Then what she was hearing began to register: her heart came to her mouth, her tongue went dry.

The man's voice was deep and sinister: 'You know where the girl is, don't you? You bugger!'

7

It was Police Constables Smith and Walsh in the house-to-house enquiry team who were allocated the more isolated farms and houses on the outskirts of Drayford.

They would have preferred the straggling road of the village proper; at least that was level, and the small cottage doors were so close together you could almost do two at once. In fact, sometimes nosy neighbours would come onto their steps at the sound of the other's door knocker, or just at the sight of a policeman through their lace-curtained windows.

Accepting their lot, the constables agreed it was not a particularly pretty village. It was the sort that one usually came upon by accident and passed through on the way to somewhere else. Even the brook that ran along one side of the road, with its bricked-up sides, an innovation for flood prevention, and little cement bridge access for cottagers, was a receptacle for the odd empty can.

There were weeds, too. Here and there miscellaneous litter probably polluted the watercress that clung to large smooth stones scarcely covered by the trickle of clear but scant summer water.

The two uniformed men left that behind and followed the lane going uphill towards the common. They parked their patrol car well in against the thick overgrown hedge. Treading carefully to avoid dogs, cats and evil-smelling brown muck that oozed between the rutted ground, they made their way across a farmyard.

Farmer Harry Patch saw them coming. He stood his ground like a squat red-faced guard outside the open farmhouse door.

'Doll!' he barked like a sergeant major. 'Come yer!'

A small, mouse-like woman appeared in a long, drab brown dress; she stayed a step behind him like a shadow.

He addressed the policemen before they reached him. ''Spect you've come to ask if us knows ought about missing maid?'

'That's right,' Walsh said. At least that saved time on preliminaries. 'Did you ever see her?'

'No. Us never, did us, Doll? When exactly did 'er go missing?' He sounded interested to hear all he could straight from what was probably the horse's mouth.

'She was last seen, as far as we know, just after nine, Wednesday evening, leaving The King's Arms.'

Constable Smith asked: 'Can you tell us where you were after that time?'

'Us were yer, o' course, weren't us, Doll?'

The mouse, her thin shoulders hunched, nodded vigorously in silent agreement.

'Can you remember seeing anything suspicious ... any stranger, or even a car go by around that time ... before or after?'

Farmer Patch rubbed his beefy hands up and down his beer gut, then smacked the distended flesh hard before pressing back his premature-stooping shoulders. He drew himself up to his full stocky height. 'Aye, us did an' all,' he said importantly, with a gleam in his hooded eyes that suggested triumph to be able to impart information. 'Aye. Us did an all,' he repeated. 'We seed someone all right, did'n us, Doll?'

He ignored the woman's vigorous nodding. 'But it weren't no stranger. It was 'er. 'Er drove down by. Did'n 'er, Doll? 'Bout ten o'clock. P'raps later.'

'Who do you mean by *her*?' Walsh asked.

''Er the maid'd come to live with. You know. Like they says in the paper.'

'Are you quite sure it was Miss Barclay?'

'Oh aye. 'Er car. Today's Friday. Come yer only last Tuesday. Go and fetch the card she dropped, Doll.'

As the woman disappeared into her mousehole he called after her, "Er name an' address an' phone number an all's on it, innit Doll?'

He turned back to the officers. 'Stuck-up little bitch. Wanted eggs. So 'er said. Then bloody changed 'er mind.' As Doll, with the silent speed of a silverfish, reappeared holding the said card, he sneered: 'Us knows 'er all right, don' us Doll? Come snoopin' in round yer, mindin' other people's business.'

The mousy head jerked up and down like a mishandled puppet.

'Did anyone else see her?' Walsh asked.

'Oh aye. 'Smatter o' fact. A rep. Our animal-feed reper prer tentative. Cow pellets an' that.' He warmed to his story, his beefy face glowing and becoming as near as it probably ever did to animation. He ran stubby fingers through his thick black curly hair "E were just about to turn into yard. Seed 'er in time as she backed out.' Farmer Patch raised his voice 'Backed out like a mazed thing, 'er did. Nasty-tempered bugger. Bloody shit.'

'I really meant, did anyone else, besides you, see her drive down by here on the night in question?'

'Doll did, didn' you Doll? I called out to 'er just as car gone by.' He slapped his paunch. 'I said fancy 'er gadding off at this time o' night, didn' I Doll?'

Walsh pressed. 'Your good lady here saw... As the car had gone by?'

'Well 'er knows the car ... an' if I told Doll it was ... Doll knows 'twas.'

'Around ten? Perhaps later? It's dark then.'

'Well, dimpsey maybe. But were 'er car.'

Walsh addressed the woman. 'And did you see?'

Startled by a direct question she looked like a rabbit caught in headlights. Simultaneously her lips clammed tightly and her head nodded, as if they were worked by the same string.

"Er knows 'twas. I told 'er,' the farmer said.

The constables exchanged glances. They concluded their

business, glad to leave the sight of neglect, the stench of dung and urine.

Their following calls included a couple of old houses set in their own grounds, and a clean, well-run farm that was a complete contrast to Farmer Patch's.

They paused to look up the drive of a long-deserted rectory said to be haunted, and which they knew had already been searched.

The large wooden gate, off its hinges, was fixed permanently open by weeds and grass, and just inside with its twisting, thick black and gnarled trunk, stood an ancient Judas tree, listed as a historical reminder of grim goings-on when Drayford and district was on the circuit of the notorious Judge Jeffreys.

Riding schools couldn't be left out, even though their owners seemed not to live on the premises. It was reasoned that, as the evenings were light until half past nine, someone might have been still around; wiping down hacks, mucking-out, or whatever else horsey types did.

Someone might have seen a stranger, or something suspicious in the maze of lanes that ran like tributaries into the one that led up to the common where Miss Barclay lived.

When they reckoned they had finished, Smith said, 'Should be something in this lot for Chief Inspector bloody Robeson to get his teeth into.'

Walsh agreed. He eased the patrol car back into the village street. 'Aye. Lucky bugger. He's working with Senior Inspector Mary Starks. Some have all the luck.'

'And Roger's working the bloody clock round, too. Reckons it's his baby because he logged first call ... when the girl didn't show up,' Smith said as they made their way back to the Incident Room.

In the Incident Room, Detective Sergeant Roger Mills had processed his notes according to custom. He had filled in forms, sent messages, and involved specialist officers who arranged search teams, house-to-house enquiry teams, and suspect teams, to work on information recorded on the questionnaires.

He knew that Superintendent John Moore, head of the CID at Divisional Headquarters was running the show, but having been first on the scene when the girl was reported missing, he staked a special interest. And some aspects were not quite as black and white as Mr Croft and Miss Barclay had made them sound.

As a result of their information, he consulted a much-used copy of the Police and Constabulary Almanac, and studied the geography of certain police areas in London South West, where the ex-Mrs Croft was said to be living.

Then he made the long distance telephone call. It would save anyone going to London, perhaps unnecessarily at this early stage, if the boys on the spot could find out about the girl from her mother.

He wanted to know what kind of a relationship they had; had she many friends; who were they; had she any enemies; had she run away before? If so, where might she go and hide?

And what about her peers at school? Was she popular? From his experience, schoolchildren when questioned were usually uninhibitedly forthcoming with gems of information.

He wished he had more time for this one; being on nights this week was a nuisance; a man had to sleep sometime, and his new wife was already facing the stark reality of what being married to an ambitious Detective Sergeant entailed.

In the meantime, he wanted a few more words with Mr Croft. He had phoned him several times yesterday. It was irritating, each time, to learn from Miss Barclay that Mr Croft was out; she was expecting him home at any minute.

Mills was not as a rule easily rattled; he prided himself on being patient, but he had other matters to attend to. His time had been already allocated for the rest of Friday.

Now, what with having been on nights, and the somewhat capricious Rest Day system, he would have to tell his long-suffering young wife that their promised Saturday jaunt was off yet again. He must speak to Jeffrey Croft.

The interview room was small; hardly surprising since it was actually the cloakroom of the village hall, but was now the best place for privacy the Incident Room could offer. When Croft came in, all six foot two of trim stature, but with exceptionally wide shoulders beneath his open-neck white shirt and light blue summer anorak, the room seemed cramped.

Mills uttered the usual bland courtesies, and had Croft take a seat on the opposite side of the table. He wasted no time on unnecessary waffle.

'Mr Croft, you said you arrived from London about ten on Wednesday night.'

'That's right. About then. I'm not sure exactly.'

'Why didn't you call the Station until two?'

'We kept hoping Kim would come in.'

'For four hours?'

'Yes.'

'Why didn't you call us while you were waiting? It was an unearthly hour for a young girl to be still out.' He looked at some papers in front of him. 'If you had informed us, and she had turned up in the meantime, well...' He shrugged. 'So much the better. Why did you wait so long?'

'I told you ... we were hoping...'

'What were you doing?'

'Talking. Waiting. Hoping.'

'For *four* hours?'

'Yes.'

'You didn't go out at all, looking for her, by yourself?'

'No.'

'Mr Croft, a couple of officers called at your house yesterday. You were out. I expect Miss Barclay told you.'

Jeffrey uncrossed his long legs. Why bother to answer the obvious?

'Why did you leave Miss Barclay alone at such a time? She seemed very upset.'

'I wanted to go into Draymouth. I'm starting with my firm's branch there, on Monday.'

Mills looked up from scribbling notes. 'It took you all day? Most offices close at five.'

'Yes. Well, I had a bit of a ride around, after.'

'Where? What were you doing?'

Croft shrugged. 'Just ... nothing particular. Driving. Thinking.'

'Were you looking for your daughter?'

'Well ... yes ... perhaps ... I suppose so.'

'But not consciously?'

'Seemed unlikely I would suddenly see her in Draymouth. I didn't expect to.'

'Why? Are you a pessimist?'

Jeffrey shrugged again, and recrossed his legs.

Mills took that for some kind of answer. 'I understand Miss Barclay expected you to arrive a bit earlier than you did, on Wednesday.'

'I set off later than I intended.'

'You told Miss Barclay there had been an accident. You didn't mention it when I asked you about your journey, and if you had passed anyone or seen anyone on the road that looked at all suspicious.'

'I didn't think it was relevant.'

'But you were very upset when you arrived?'

'Well, yes. Who wouldn't be? An accident.'

'Were you involved? What exactly ... a car, lorry, or what? Were there police, ambulance, any other witnesses besides yourself?'

'I didn't see it, I mean not to witness, I think it was a car, I don't know.' He shifted his sitting position, as if he

65

needed the snatched moment to recollect. 'There was a car stopped in front of me, I backed up and made a detour, away from the main road.'

'Where exactly did this accident happen?'

'I don't know. Not exactly, I ... I think this side of Taunton. It was dark.'

'It's not really dark until ten. That's when you say you arrived home.'

'I did. Well, it was getting dark, and I don't know the road that well.'

'And you knew the minor road, to detour?'

'Not really. I took a chance.'

'Mr Croft, four years ago you were sentenced to six months for driving offences and banned from driving for two years.' Mills spoke moderately, on his own premise that it brought better results in the early stages of an enquiry, than if you rode the high horse. 'Is that why you withheld the information?'

'No. It is not.' Jeffrey swore under his breath. What the hell! 'It was irrelevant,' he said emphatically, anger rising. 'It was irrelevant, because I was not involved.'

'Were you particularly careful *not* to mention it? After all, you did kill a man by reckless driving?'

'What's that got to do with this?' Jeffrey snapped. 'Why's that being dragged up?' He leaned towards Mills over the table. 'I paid the price, didn't I? Maybe I had had one drink when it happened, as you seem to know it all.' He shook with indignation. 'Just one drink, mark you! No one would have known but for the scruff who lurched from nowhere in front of my car.' He glared angrily at the young detective. 'And he was pissed out of his mind!'

Mills said nothing. Let the man talk, you could learn a lot when hackles were up.

Jeffrey lowered his voice as if speaking to himself. 'I paid one Hell of a price, and I've been paying ever since.' His lips stiffened. 'I thought, coming here to live, I'd have a clean slate, be allowed to forget, get away from the threats.'

'Threats, Mr Croft?'

Jeffrey realised with a jerk, thinking aloud, perhaps he had said too much. He looked at Mills.

Mills waited. Then, 'Threats, Mr Croft?'

Jeffrey sighed his resignation. Reluctantly he enlarged. 'The boy's father attacked me as I was leaving court. Thought the sentence inadequate.' He shifted his position again. 'He's made my life hell ever since. I'd killed his son. He vowed he'd get me!'

'How has he made your life hell?'

'Dozens of ways. Character assassination. I couldn't socialise. Or join a club. He made things too unpleasant.' Jeffrey looked across at the small, frosted-glass window. 'He made sure I was an embarrassment. And there were always the threats. So I transferred down here.'

'Who is this man, where does he live?'

'What odds? He's all talk. His boy was blind drunk. It was proved.' Jeffrey shrugged, and paused before going on. 'But I'd already had a couple of driving offences. That was the trouble. I panicked.'

He looked straight at Mills. 'Wouldn't you panic if someone suddenly lurched in front of you and you drove several yards with him on the bonnet?'

Mills didn't answer. Jeffrey pushed back his wide shoulders as if to ease them; he was too tall for the chair. 'I don't want to recall the boy's father, his name, or anything about him. I just want to forget.'

Mills pondered.

Jeffrey added, 'If only people will let me.'

Mills glanced at some papers. 'Any disturbance in court will be in the Press records; I can get most of the facts from official sources.' He paused, then asked suddenly, 'Why did you go outside the house while you were waiting? Miss Barclay said you were gone some time.'

Jeffrey was momentarily floored. 'I didn't. I mean I wasn't. Not out a long time.' He hesitated. 'I wasn't out more than five or ten minutes. We thought we heard someone outside.'

'What time would that have been?'

'God knows. Never noticed. Can't remember. Probably around eleven.'

'Why didn't you mention it when I came on Wednesday night, or rather, the early hours of Thursday?'

'Never thought any more about it. We had thought we heard Kim. When she didn't come in, I went outside to look.'

'And that's when you were a long time? What were you doing in your five or ten minutes?'

'I walked up and down. Looked over the hedge. There was a fair amount of light from the house.'

'Did you see anything ... anyone walking?'

'No. It was pretty dark away from the house.' He paused. 'Now ... come to think of it ... I did just catch sight of a car.'

Mills looked wide-eyed with surprise.

Jeffrey said, 'I remember. I saw the red tail lights disappearing down round the bend in the lane.'

Mills was incredulous. 'And you didn't think that was important enough to mention when I came?'

'Raine said the occasional car does go by. Probably courting couples, she said. Been up on the common.'

'What time was that?'

'I can't remember. As I said. Probably elevenish.'

The probing went on. At Mill's request, a duty constable brought them both a cup of tea. Jeffrey felt drained. He didn't resent recounting his exact route home, but his motor offence was history and he felt it should have remained so. He should have been allowed a fresh start; kept the past hidden, like rust under new paint.

At last there were no more questions. 'For the time being,' Mills said. He had no grounds to keep Croft any longer. Perhaps what he'd said would link with other reports. Investigative teams were working on information gleaned from the uniformed officers' house-to-house teams. And public help had been enlisted to search the area over the weekend.

* * *

68

On Sunday, the village was buzzing. Hundreds of policemen, many with sniffer dogs, had been drafted in. They were joined by most of the local able-bodied population eager to help. They tramped through the village, over the fields, through the lanes. They beat the hedges, peered in ponds and ditches. They searched farms, old sheds, barns, and stables.

Raine and Jeffrey took a different direction from the organised groups, preferring to avoid recognition; perhaps being assailed by the over-sympathetic, or the overtly inquisitive. They didn't speak much; everything they had wanted to say, had been said. They walked, locked in their separate silences.

Raine thought about the anonymous phone call. Was it yesterday? She had been frozen. Terrified. As if there was someone outside the window watching her, perhaps even enjoying her reaction.

She had kept the horror to herself, told no one, and willed herself to keep calm. After hours alone, with Jeffrey still in Draymouth, she had forced herself to think rationally.

She refused to panic. She understood there were always sick people around to molest you at times like these. The call was better not mentioned. Jeffrey would tell the police and she couldn't stand more probing. The call, with its implication, might get blown up, and there was always someone who would quote 'There's no smoke without fire'.

She paced alongside Jeff in silence, going through the motions of looking for Kim. After several hours, she was thankful when he put his arm around her shoulder, and gently turned her towards home.

Normally, there would be the Sunday papers to read. But she had tidied them away, not wanting to see any more headlines and long detailed reports of Kim's disappearance.

Every scrap of information, however trivial, was being followed up by investigating teams.

Even the television news, when they switched on, included:

Concern is mounting for the whereabouts of the fourteen-year-old schoolgirl, Kim Croft, who has been missing for the past four days from her home in Drayford, where she had recently gone to live with her father.

Monica must have supplied a photo. Kim, smiling, in black and white; almond-shaped eyes, tiny coiled springs of hair framing her thin face.

Jeffrey blew his nose and switched off.

There were several hours of daylight left, but they stayed indoors. Tomorrow he would go to his new office; if anyone wanted him Raine knew where he could be found. There was nothing he could do here.

Raine was tired. But that night, again she couldn't sleep. In the early hours of Monday, just as it was getting light, she got up and went into the garden.

The common looked peaceful. The strip of silver sea in the distance was flat and calm. As she observed the gentle light on the water, she thought that that same sea was like the village of Drayford, whose innocent surface belied the depths beneath.

She cut several blooms of her favourite yellow roses. It was a pity to watch them blow, and she wanted to stay indoors when the search of the common was resumed.

In little more time than it took her to arrange the flowers carefully in her crystal rose-bowl she heard the helicopters. Then they were almost above her.

She looked from the drawing-room window. Police were gathering; dark blue specks converging onto the common like flies onto a dung heap. Police on horseback. Police with tracker dogs.

She drew the long gold velvet curtains, careful to let no chink of light into the room from that dreadful world outside.

She pummelled and rearranged her embroidered chair cushions for the hundredth time, as if by moving her limbs she could halt her mind, forget the past, the present, and all the conjecture of what might lie ahead.

She made coffee, and cooked breakfast for Jeffrey.

70

Afterwards, he kissed her, held her tightly and, before leaving for Draymouth, promised to ring.

'Just to know you're all right, darling. But don't forget. If you want me I'm only at the end of the line.'

It sounded so easy; he had already switched off; detached himself from their predicament by going to work. How could he?

She felt trapped. She wouldn't go out alone, with no support; she hadn't had time to make friends, she was still a stranger. There would be furtive nudges and glances. People would stop talking if she went in the Post Office. Already some would probably be whispering 'Murder'.

She heard Ginger outside. The kitchen window was open. Gently she drew the brightly-patterned cotton curtains a little closer together. He would probably finish the painting this week. She wouldn't ask.

Time dragged. It was nearly mid-morning when the phone rang. She sighed with relief; thank goodness, Jeff; someone to talk to. She picked up the receiver. 'Jeff?'

Silence. Then she heard the same sinister voice as before. 'You know where she is, you bugger.'

She dropped the phone. It hung swinging on its coil. Her heart hammered. Who knew her number? It was not in the directory. She heard the instrument whirring; stared at it for several moments. Gingerly, as if it might bite her, she put it back on its rest.

Almost at once, it rang again. She let it ring. And ring. And ring. Shaking, she threw herself onto a chair in the darkened drawing room.

Exhausted from fear, and her wakeful night, eventually she fell asleep.

She woke to find Jeffrey standing beside her.

'So that's why you didn't answer the phone!' He wrapped his arms around her. 'My God, darling, I'm sorry! I never realised you were so flaked!'

She clung to him.

He said: 'I've been ringing for ages. And I wondered if you had heard the news. They've found a body.'

71

8

Raine went cold. They had found a body, and she felt too sick to utter what her whole being screamed inside. When, how, where?

With shaking fingers she took the brandy that Jeffrey poured for her. It burned her throat and nearly took her breath away; but her mind had frozen as if its numbness provided a protective barrier against what she was afraid to hear.

She controlled herself, sipping the spirit more slowly. Jeffrey added nothing to the news, his concern for her diverted by the chimes of the doorbell. He gave her shoulder a supportive squeeze before he answered.

She heard voices and instinctively knew they were the police again, even before Jeffrey ushered them into the darkened drawing room. He drew back the curtains with a rough flourish.

'Raine had a headache,' he said, as if explanation were needed.

Brilliant sunshine poured through the closed window.

She recognised the tall, thickset Chief Inspector Howard Robeson. He had called before; she felt she had already spent enough time looking at that curly brown hair and those restless dark eyes. With him again was the neat, quietly-dressed Inspector Mary Starks whose demure good looks made you wonder what was going on in that head of short, honey-coloured hair.

Inert, Raine supposed they were probably wondering why she didn't open the window if she had a headache. Perhaps they were immune to the sound of helicopters.

She didn't get up from her armchair. The Inspector

looked at her with a mere flicker of his thick lips, which she took to mean that he understood. With a move of his hand he declined Jeffrey's invitation to sit down. Inspector Starks stood at attention beside him.

Raine thought, surely no more questions. They already knew where and when she was born; where Jeffrey was born, when he was married and to whom; when the marriage broke down, and when and where Kim was born.

They had asked her some of the same questions over and over again. Besides which, the CID, like some giant octopus, was spreading tentacles of enquiry teams throughout Monica's district in London; among Kim's schoolfriends and acquaintances. What more?

'We would like to have another look at the girl's room, Miss Barclay,' Inspector Robeson said quietly.

God. Not again. Not even please. Damn room. Looks awful.

She went with them. Jeffrey stayed downstairs, told rather pointedly by the Inspector that he wasn't needed. She had always thought that one of the most depressing sights was a badly-made bed. That dislike probably stemmed from her childhood spent amid Aunt Jo's domestic chaos. Now, despite her resolve that her own home would be different, Kim's unkempt room looked a shambles.

As the three of them stood in the room that had three walls covered in posters of garish gyrating figures, and horrific faces grimacing in seeming agony, Robeson asked:

'And you haven't touched anything, have you?'

'No,' Raine said. It was only a small lie, she had tidied very little. She couldn't have been expected to leave Kim's pants lying inside out where they had been discarded on the floor.

She wondered if they noticed her slight hesitation. The other woman's steady brown eyes looked so innocent; but they were probably alert to every detail, like that obsessively vigilant Detective Sergeant Mills, the first one who came.

'Have you discovered yet if she took anything; any money,

73

any clothes other than what she was wearing? A photograph perhaps, or a favourite possession?' Robeson asked.

Raine hadn't done any sleuth work, what difference would it make? The girl wasn't here. Everything else looked the same. She felt the man watching her, waiting for some kind of response.

Her eyes rested on the large yellow holdall still lying on the bed. This was the bag which in her confusion on that first night she had said Kim had taken, but Detective Sergeant Mills's sharp eyes had seen.

Since then, in spite of her obsession for order she had, under instructions, been afraid to touch anything, apart from her compulsion to pick up Kim's knickers from the floor.

Now, with sudden wonder dawning and prompted by something Inspector Robeson had said, she went towards the bag and pushed her hands against the firm canvas sides. They hollowed in.

She looked round at the officer, hesitant. 'She ... she may have ... she must have taken her Sony.' It sounded a sudden revelation. Raine knew of course she shouldn't be surprised, but why hadn't she thought of it before? 'She used to take it everywhere. In here sometimes, but sometimes she carried it with a strap from her shoulder.'

'And this is the first time you've reported it?'

'I hadn't noticed before.' She supposed it sounded lame after all the times she had been asked to note if there was anything missing.

'Can you describe it? What was it exactly, a radio, a cassette player, or what? How big, what colour?'

'It was a Sony. She always called it her Sony. It was a stereo radio cassette. Black.'

'How big?'

Raine paused to think. 'It was ... about eighteen inches wide,' she said, holding her hands apart to indicate its size. 'Clumsy. Really big. And hard,' she added remembering all the places where it had been bumped against, and had marked the freshly decorated walls and doors.

Robeson was leaving any note-taking to his assistant. He changed the subject.

'Was she happy? I mean here with you?'

'Yes. I think so.'

'You said she preferred to go out on her own. Understandable, I've got a teenager myself.' His restless eyes finished their sweep of the room and met hers. 'Had she made any special friend, or an acquaintance since she had been here?'

Raine only knew the very little that Kim had told her. And Kim told lies. She exaggerated, and boasted. Would it be right to implicate the 'William' that Kim had fancied and been determined to meet and speak to? Even if she had succeeded in doing so, he certainly would have been impervious to Kim's unsubtle approach, if his reputation as Bible Billy were true.

'She went into Draymouth last Saturday. Came back on the last bus.' Raine felt sure it had no relevance, but it showed her co-operation. 'She said she hitched a lift up the lane. Some fella.'

'Did she tell you anything about him?'

'Nothing at all.'

'And you didn't ask? A young girl like that? Out so late, accepting a lift by a stranger?'

'Well, no. She didn't like me asking questions.'

'But you got on well, you said.'

'Yes ... but ... she was at an awkward age.'

'Was?'

'Is' Raine corrected, remembering Sergeant Mills's impatience with her use of the past tense, and aware of Inspector Starks, scribbling. These people lived in a world where dots, commas, and tenses were measured, time and details obsessively noticed; where the flick of an eyelid, the tremor in a voice, was an alert to be noted.

'Has she seen him since, did she make a date?'

'She never said. But she came home from Draymouth by taxi on Tuesday. It was late.'

'Do you happen to know whose taxi?'

'No.'

'And you don't know of anyone who might bear her a grudge?'

'No.' She heard Kim's voice in her mind relating her conquests over Monica's boyfriends and how the one she accused of indecency, when he wouldn't play ball, had vowed to get her one day. 'No,' Raine repeated. 'She only arrived last Thursday week.'

'And you had no kind of quarrel?'

'No.'

'Or no words that perhaps she might have taken exception to?'

'No.' Raine's cheeks burned. Why tell the truth if it was irrelevant and would only complicate matters?

Robeson looked at Inspector Starks. Raine thought it indicated he had finished his probing, but he strode to the window, looked out over the lane and hedges, and across the fields. 'Wonderful outlook you have here. And from the other side of the house. Over the common. Glorious.' He paused. 'Damn good country for anyone to hide.'

What did he mean to imply? She wondered.

'I see you're having the outside painted. How long has the painter been coming?'

'This is the third week.'

'Then he would have seen Mr Croft's daughter?'

'Yes.'

'You weren't perhaps jealous of her? Wanted her out of the way? Maybe you didn't want her, and a baby, too?'

She almost jumped, staggered by his suggestion and its lack of truth. 'I'm not having a baby!'

'But you told the painter, didn't you?'

'No!'

Her whole being burned with indignation. Was nothing of her personal life to be left alone? Was her every past utterance to be exposed to question?

'No, I didn't; I mean yes, but not really,' she corrected, realising it was useless to deny what Ginger had obviously divulged under questioning.

76

She felt the officers watching her like spiders with their web, waiting for a fly. 'I only said about a baby, to explain why I wanted this room decorated with nursery motifs ... it ... was ... just in case ... later.'

Robeson's thick lips twitched. She assumed he believed her. He moved to the door, and aside for her to go downstairs first.

She felt drained. It was a relief when at last they drove off. She wondered who had questioned Ginger, and when? She supposed it was during the house-to-house. He would have had to say he was working here, which would have marked him for deeper questioning. But what exactly had he said, apart from the quite natural misunderstanding about the baby?

She was tempted to draw the curtains over again, shut out the light, the sight of mounted police, and uniformed men with tracker dogs that were still out there on the common.

But what was the use? She must just force herself not to look, and in any case why were they still out there, and why hadn't the Inspector said anything about their having found a body?

What were they playing at? They hadn't taken her away. Only asked questions. If Jeffrey could carry on without going to pieces, she must try.

She accepted with inward gratitude that Jeffrey apparently wasn't going to upset her again with more of the news he'd come home to tell her. She didn't want to hear it, as if as long as she didn't, it didn't concern her.

She drank the cup of strong coffee Jeffrey made.

He said: 'Let's go for a drive. Get away from the village for a few hours. Have a run over Dartmoor.'

But even to leave the village, it seemed to her they had to run some kind of gauntlet. At intervals down the lane, there were stakes in the hedge with blown-up pictures of Kim, headlined *Have You Seen This Girl?* The same posters appeared in the windows of the Post Office, The Kings Arms, and private cottages; on walls, and on the iron rail-

77

ings alongside the brook that ran down one side of the street. On the main road copies were being handed out to passing motorists.

They drove for miles in silence. Raine supposed Jeff had his mind on the road, traffic was heavy. The peak holiday season had brought many motorists unaccustomed to the south west's narrow lanes. They needed constantly to reverse, or pull into passing-bays as they climbed their winding way up and over cattle-grids to the moor.

Jeffrey suggested, as if this was all that had been on his mind for the past half hour: 'Raine, why not ask your Aunt Jo to come and stay for a while?'

She turned to look at him. He kept his eyes ahead. 'Aunt Jo! God, Jeffrey!'

'But you're fond of her...'

'I know. To a point' she conceded, thoroughly put out by the mere suggestion. 'Not to live with. She's eccentric.'

'It would be company.'

'I couldn't.'

'But I can't keep leaving work as I have now, wondering how you are. I'd know you weren't alone.'

'Maybe. But...' The thought of domestic upheaval dismayed her. 'Anyway, where can she sleep? We can't touch the spare room.'

'Just till things blow over.'

'Blow over?' Raine had been bemused by his non-reaction to events, secretly relieved by his stoicism, but for all the sensitivity in that remark he might have been dismissing a tiff with neighbours.

He eased up. Then he practically stopped; a sheep that had been hidden in the shadow of the raised grizzled edge of the moor, ambled across the road in front of him.

He drove on carefully, mindful of more sheep that looked about to do the same. 'There's a settee-bed in the drawing room.'

'God! Jo would make the room look Hell in five minutes. She's so untidy, Jeffrey. You'd never believe.'

'Dammit, what does that matter?'

78

'It would drive me mad.'

'It's you,' he said irritably, 'you're too damn fussy.'

It wasn't fair. She already felt at breaking point. It wouldn't be him at home all day with Aunt Jo, seeing nothing ever put straight, let alone put away.

He turned off the road into an open space, and parked a short distance from some other cars. People had laid out their picnics, and an ice-cream van near the entrance to the gap was doing good business.

They sat in uneasy silence. All around them the high rolling landscape reached away into the distance until it was a mauve haze that merged with a skyline pierced here and there by dark granite tors.

'Raine,' Jeffrey said at last. 'The settee will have to be used. Monica wants to come down.'

'Monica?'

'She rang me. She must come. It's understandable.'

'God yes. Of course, Jeff. When? Why didn't you tell me before?'

'I meant to. But there was so much else. Then those police again.'

They agreed on the subject of Monica. But the idea that they could temporarily escape the shadow cast by Kim, by fleeing the village of Drayford, was short-lived. Her disappearance had made the national press. The nearby picnickers, seated on chairs they had brought with them, were mostly reading the tabloids. Raine saw headlines: EXPELLED SCHOOLGIRL MISSING, and HAVE YOU SEEN HER? over a smiling, out-of-date picture of Kim.

Some litter lout had actually dropped one of the village leaflets with Kim's more accurate likeness. It inched slowly along the uneven ground in sporadic hops until it clung to a clump of gorse at the side of the clearing.

It was the first that Raine knew of Kim having been expelled from school. She wasn't surprised, though she wouldn't tackle Jeffrey about it just now.

Without rancour she accepted that naturally Monica must come down. After hearing her daughter was missing,

79

and being interviewed in London, Monica would probably want to join in the search. Raine was surprised she hadn't come at once.

They had met briefly on only two occasions, but there was no animosity between them. Raine's impression of Monica was of someone rather too sweet; smooth and crisp like a meringue, with nothing inside.

She remembered Monica's easygoing, take-it-or-leave-it attitude to everything; the demerara-coloured hair, and blue almond-shaped eyes so like Kim's.

Raine sighed. The way she was feeling now, she could have done with a different sort of company, not someone who was all promise but no substance, with the kind of concentration lost as easily as a dandelion clock in the breeze. Though for certain now, Kim's disappearance would have made a sobering difference.

Raine saw some scruffy ponies coming into the clearing. Picnics were hurriedly scooped up and got out of their way. One animal came to her side of the car, put its head against the window, its yellow teeth and inquisitive brown eyes with straight black lashes, just inches away. Normally she would have got out and patted it, nuzzled its head, stroked its untidy mane. She didn't bother to move and, after a few moments, disappointed at no response, it moved away and started to lick the bonnet.

The car needs a damn good wash, she thought idly; inside was a mess too; old dusters, road maps, and the locker full of bits and pieces. Jeffrey never cleared it out.

She wanted to leave here. It seemed pointless sitting in heavy silence, surrounded by holiday-makers enjoying themselves.

As Jeffrey drove back across the moor, she was in no mood to appreciate the rugged tors outlined against the sky; the wild ponies foraging among the rolling expanse of scrub and heather. At intervals cattle-grids rattled beneath them, jolting her from closing her eyes, tired after so many sleepless nights.

They passed fields of cattle, black-faced sheep, warders

on horseback near the granite prison, and the radio masts of Hessary Tor that seemed to disappear into low drifting clouds.

She began to relax, dozed in fits and starts, and for a few blissful moments forgot the CID, the police Incident Room in the village hall, and thoughts of officers going through lists of statements.

So she was shattered, on arrival home, to find Inspector Robeson waiting.

9

Inspector Howard Robeson's business with Raine didn't take long, but left him in a seething temper.

After seeing her he drove as fast he dare down the narrow lane to the Incident Room in the village hall. Inspector Starks sat in silent sympathy beside him.

He was a tall, well-built man in his late forties, with a mop of curly brown hair showing grey in front of his ears. Although he had a decent home to go to, and a wife ready to cook and attend to his every want, he seldom had much chance to appreciate such luck. And since Kim Croft had gone missing he had certainly had no time to indulge his hobby of birdwatching. It was the only pursuit that gave him the occasional chance to really relax and unwind. He reckoned it was over two weeks since he had joined his fellow enthusiasts in their hide on the Dray estuary.

He had his own organised office at Divisional Headquarters where he supervised, checked files, directed, and worked with adrenalin-charged enthusiasm. Now he was a familiar face in Drayford, too. And it pleased him that he already knew many of the officers that had been drafted to work in the recently set-up Incident Room. Some were from his own department and several came from Draymouth Police Station. He had been in the force years longer than any of them and, even allowing for accepted rules of behaviour of individual ranks, owing to his wide experience he frequently got away with his occasional assumption that he was a law unto himself.

He left Inspector Starks to park the Sierra in the limited space left between other police cars, and marched straight into the building that with its corrugated sides he regarded as no more than a shack. It seemed they could possibly have two big jobs on their hands now. Even with the two hundred extra manpower drafted in, they were already stretched, and that damn Barclay girl had been less than helpful to say the least. In fact she had been questionably devious.

There were a number of detectives working in the room when he burst in.

'Any of you chaps seen any daylight yet?'

'Missing girl, sir, or the lad found hanged?' Several men had spoken at once.

'The girl for starters.'

'Nearly two thousand statements, sir. Around five thousand interviews. That's so far.'

Robeson fixed his restless dark eyes on Detective Sergeant Roger Mills who had supplied the information. 'I said daylight, Roger. I know we've got a whole bloody army out there making routine enquiries.'

'Every scrap's being followed up by investigating teams, sir. Statements being read and cross-referenced.'

'Well I'm in a bloody fog myself and it gets thicker,' Robeson said, commanding attention. 'That bloody Barclay girl. The times I've quizzed her!' He rested on the corner of a desk and crossed his long legs. 'She answers only what she's asked, and that after a fashion. I'm wondering how much more she's holding back.'

He turned his head briefly as Mary Starks came into the room. 'This morning ... only this morning mind you ... she tells me the girl was carrying a large Sony radio. Fresh bulletins had to be put out.' He uncrossed his legs and stood up. 'Then a farmer tells Constables Smith and Walsh that Barclay's car went down Moor lane past his place last Wednesday night around ten.' He took a deep breath and blew it out with exasperation. 'I tackled her about it. Just half an hour ago. She calmly said she sold it. Last Wednesday. About ten.' His voice rose. 'Jesus Christ! Never a dicky bird about this before. She didn't think it relevant.'

'We've had three reports of a car seen in the vicinity of

83

Moor Lane on Wednesday night, sir,' Roger Mills said. 'But they weren't mentioned when I went to the house at 2 a.m. on Thursday. After I was called.'

'Did you ask?' Robeson snapped.

'I asked everything in the book, sir, and some.' He reached for a file. 'It took an interview with Croft on Saturday before he casually admitted he had seen the rear lights of a car disappearing down Moor Lane.'

'What time?'

'Around eleven.'

'Not ten?'

'No, sir.'

'We've got another statement on that one, sir,' Detective Constable Mike Searle put in.

'Any ideas?'

'Yes. Someone rang in. Wouldn't give his name. Saw a van in Moor Lane about eleven. He recognised it. A local painter and decorator's.'

'And that fits,' Sergeant Mills said. 'Croft saw rear lights around eleven.'

'A local chap? Has he been questioned?'

Mike Searle referred to papers in front of him. 'A Gordon Anthony Retter. Known as Ginger Retter in the village. Does contract work for a small Draymouth firm of builders.'

'Didn't the uniform men call on him on their routine house-to-house?' Robeson asked.

'Yes, sir. Questionnaire's here. But he never said he was near Miss Barclay's place on Wednesday night.' Searle paused. 'Only that he knew the missing girl. By sight. He's working at the house.'

'Jesus Christ.' Robeson raised his eyes to the ceiling. 'I remember. I sifted that one. He said Miss Barclay's a lovely lady, and she's having a baby.' He drew a chair from under a desk, sat down, and indicated Inspector Starks to do the same.

'I'll see Mr Retter. I hope his next story's more reliable. He got it all wrong about the baby.' Robeson glanced

84

around at his subordinates; at fresh faces not yet hardened by contact with violent crime, at eyes he hoped would always remain as keen and alert. 'First. One of you....' His gaze rested on DC Searle. 'You, Mike. Get on to Swansea.' He took a notebook from the breast pocket of his impeccably white shirt. 'You want particulars of this man. That's the car number,' he indicated, handing over the open book. 'You want them *now*. At once! Not at their bureaucratic speed.' He pulled a face and shook his head from side to side. A lock of curly brown hair fell over his broad forehead. 'Who would believe it! That Barclay girl sold her car and doesn't even know the man's name or address. So she says.' He threw out his large hands, palms upwards in despair. 'She just handed over the documents. No questions. No cheque. Took cash. Two thousand. In grubby twenty-pound notes.'

There was a general stirring among the men. Although it seemed Robeson sometimes poked his nose in when they were working flat out, most of them understood him. He'd often complained he had spent years handling bread-and-butter jobs on his way to promotion. Petty frauds, trivial thefts, and minor crimes seemed never to have reached him until they'd been well gone over and were stale. Now as Chief Inspector it was obvious he couldn't resist chivvying if he thought there were important matters that might not be reaching him quickly enough.

His job did not include doing everyone else's. But no one seemed to resent his intrusions. And he valued all ranks as private sources of relevant gossip. He had been a policeman too long to discount the odd titbits, the occasional character assassinations, and domestic biographies overheard in pubs or via the grapevine. He said:

'This girl. Any picture from the locals?'

'No one knew her, sir.' Mills said. 'Not to speak to. According to some, she wore her skirt up to her arse.'

Robeson wanted more than that. He tried not to sound impatient as he dismissed the remark with a curt, 'The fashion, I believe. Where she comes from.'

Mills added, 'Apparently she couldn't take her eyes off men. Can't,' he corrected himself to the present tense. 'Apparently she ogled every male in the church. Last Sunday week, that was.' He paused. 'Seems she made one woman furious because,' he paused again and grinned, 'the woman said her old man's at a funny age, whatever that meant.' He flicked through some papers for reference. 'And in the reports from London, comments gathered from acquaintances, school peers, teachers, and such ... she sounds a right spoiled little brat.'

Robeson wanted motives. With sickening recollection he knew in some cases there were none. 'Being a spoilt brat's no reason for someone to whisk her away.'

Mills said: 'Perhaps she hasn't been. Maybe she's hiding somewhere. Just to cause trouble. She sounds a rebel.'

'Then where is she? Even rebels have to eat, Roger.' Robeson didn't share Mills's optimism. After five days of a full scale intensive search, with pictures and bulletins issued nationwide; TV, radio, and national Press coverage, he was mindful of possibilities and statistics. Just as he was fully aware that now there were many among the general public who were beginning to whisper, 'Murder.' Schizophrenics murdered innocent people. Eighty per cent of murders were spur of the moment. July and August were the worst months for sex murders, when children were on holiday.

He shrugged off negative thoughts, the sin of defeatism. There was no indication the girl had been murdered, the Incident Room was still receiving daily phone calls from people with news which they thought might help. Admittedly, some came from cranks, others from self-styled mediums. Many were anonymous. One eccentric had had a vision; the beautiful fourteen-year-old with the bubbly fair hair had turned into a mermaid and was lying on the bed of the Bristol channel.

Apart from the nutters and time-wasters, all calls however unlikely had to be followed up. Robeson squared his broad shoulders to face the fact that every day the name of yet another possible suspect appeared on his desk.

He turned his attention from the men now busily poring over their papers, and looked towards the door. His immediate boss, Superintendent Moore came in; it was his second appearance of the day.

'Sir,' Robeson acknowledged him. 'I was just about to deal with this other case, the boy found hanged. It's local.'

'I'm well informed, Howard.' Immediately taking over, Moore's glance swivelled round the room until his eyes rested on Inspector Mary Starks. 'Well now, Inspector Starks...' He was sometimes less formal with Mary when they were working together, but never let her forget his position, and in front of the men always addressed her by her rank. 'This other job. Distressed parents are your forte.'

'You mean the parents of the lad that's hanged himself?'

'The coroner will decide by whose hand a healthy young man came to be hanging from a tree,' Moore rebuked.

Several men hid tightened lips behind their hands. Most of them thought the thirty-year-old senior detective was a *dish*. Those who knew her before she was promoted on her record of intelligence, discretion, and above average common sense, were glad she'd stayed every inch feminine. Moore was damn lucky to have her in the team.

She showed no resentment at what some would have considered a snub. 'Going to be a bit tricky, isn't it sir?'

'You implying his death's linked to the girl?'

'No, sir. Though it is possible. Some will say obvious.'

'Some will say anything. Where's the girl? You suggesting he took her with him? Buried her perhaps, beneath the tree?' Moore's sarcasm came across as strongly as his voice. 'Anyway, she's been gone six days. The boy's death was this morning. There's nothing yet to suggest any connection.' He paused. 'We don't want rumours, we want facts. Now Inspector Starks ... I know how well you can deal with distraught mothers.' He looked at Robeson: 'Do you think there's any connection, Howard?'

'Can't say, sir. The news has already broken. Be in this evening's rag, for certain. I suppose then we'll start hearing things. The boy's parents may be pestered. Might like protection.'

As Robeson spoke, the door opened and Detective Sergeant Brian Jones came in. 'Protection? Who? Have I missed something?'

Superintendent Moore answered; his disciplined impatience was obvious in his clipped briefing. 'Parents of boy found hanged this morning. Doctor said dead four or five hours. Reported to coroner.'

'Identified, sir?'

'Local. Village bobby Trevor Drew was called out. Later our chaps took a Mrs Pym to the mortuary. She signed a statement it was her son.'

'What do we know of him?'

'Full name William John Pym. Aged twenty. No regular job. A loner. Sidesman at the Drayford Church.'

'Thanks, sir. Seems we could've got a right little can of worms.' Jones went to his own desk.

There was a general riffling of papers.

Mills teased for all to hear, 'We think he may have taken the girl with him.'

Moore glared. But he knew more about his subordinates than their records showed; he considered Mills's nosyparker mind was an asset. He was also reliable, well-read, and dedicated to his job, with the bonus of being happily married. Too many men in the department, like himself, had broken marriages they blamed on pressures of the job.

He addressed Robeson: 'I want you to go and see Mr and Mrs Pym, Howard. Find out if the boy left a note. Any gem that might help the inquest.' He glanced from him to Mary and back. 'Inspector Starks will go with you.'

Robeson frowned. He wanted to concentrate on his leads on the missing girl, and going to the Pym's seemed a diversion.

Moore said: 'You're not one of those chaps who think women police officers should be kept for dealing with lost children and baby snatchers, are you?'

Robeson glanced at the slim, neatly dressed Inspector

Starks, an assistant worth having when the presence of a female officer was necessary. 'No sir. It's just that I'm on my way to see a Mr Anthony Retter, down the village.'

Moore looked from one to the other. 'Well Howard, you and Inspector Starks can see Mr and Mrs Pym afterwards. It's still not far in the village. Then go up to the riding school. Get a clearer account of this morning's discovery, before the Press mangle it.' He added as an afterthought. 'And have a word to check it with Constable Drew at the Drayford Police House.'

Robeson never aimed to attract attention. It suited his calling to dress in fawn cord trousers and, according to the weather, a rather crumpled navy jacket over a clean white shirt. He was sufficiently self-assured to know his casual appearance belied a quick brain; a gift of insight that saw through the devious, many-sided answers he sometimes received in response to his questions.

Rather than draw up in his conspicuous car, he went on foot to look for his next subject for interrogation. He noticed The King's Arms, open all day, on the right-hand side of the church, had already attracted customers. He hoped as he passed, that his face and large build wouldn't draw attention. A hundred yards or so further on, on the same side of the road, but to the left of the church, he found the cottage he was looking for. It was one of a short terrace facing a hedged field. Outside the door stood a small blue van with a sign on its side, G.A. RETTER. PAINTER AND DECORATOR.

Robeson knocked as discreetly as he could. The heavy brass knocker, shaped like a horse's head, was well polished and he was careful not to lift it too high and let it fall with a bang.

The door was opened at once.

'Good afternoon. Mr Retter?'

Ginger nodded, his eyes wide.

'I'm Detective Chief Inspector Howard Robeson. CID.' Before he could say more, Ginger gave him what he supposed was a silent invitation by backing away from the door and keeping aside to make room for him to pass. He went in, careful not to knock his head on the low lintel.

The precise little room was so small he took it in at a glance; the square table dead centre, covered with a brocade cloth; four wooden chairs, a small armchair each side of an old-fashioned black hearth, china dogs on the high mantelpiece. The smell of paint and boiling washing billowed in with a cloud of steam from the adjoining kitchen.

It was surprising, thought Robeson, what you could take in at a glance if your brain moved at the speed of your optic nerve; the young painter was biting his lips as he clumsily dragged chairs from beneath the table for them to sit on.

'Mr Retter,' Robeson began, anxious to waste no time when it looked to him as if the young man was about to pass out at any moment. 'Can you tell me where you were on Wednesday evening, the thirty-first of July?'

'Aw ... Aw. I was working.'

'I mean in the evening after nine thirty.'

'Aw. Well. Then. Working. Odd jobs. Here. Pickin' up an' that. And ... I ... I sometimes watch telly.'

'You didn't go out?' Robeson faced him across the table.

'Aw.' Ginger thought aloud, dragging out the word, 'Wednesday?'

Robeson prompted Retter's slow thinking. 'You didn't by any chance go out in your van, say, perhaps around eleven o'clock?'

Ginger thought again. Then his pale eyes widened and his hand flew to his mouth. 'Aw. Yes. I ... I did. I switched off the telly. 'Twas something noisy. I went outside for a breath of air before turning in. And...' He paused as if the recollection still surprised him. 'Th ... they'd took me ladder.'

'Who had?'

Ginger shrugged. 'V ... vandals I s'ppose. From off me van.'

'Didn't you hear them? Did you report it?'

'Aw. No. I had the telly on. But I went to l ... look for

it.' He paused. 'I thought I... I must have left it up at the house.'

'What house?' Robeson asked.

'Mmm ... Moor Lane. Where I'm painting. Mmm ... Miss Barclay's.'

'What time was that?'

'Aw. I don't know ... P ... p'raps after eleven.'

'Dark to go looking for a ladder, wasn't it?'

'Aw. There was lots o' lights on ... at the house ... an' windows open.'

'Did you ring the door bell? See anyone? Let Miss Barclay know what you were doing?'

'Aw. No. He was there. S ... s ... so I just looked round for it.'

'Who's he, and how did you know he was there?'

'Aw. Mmm ... Miss Barclay's er ... fff ... fiancé. Sh ... she said he was coming. His cc ... car was outside.'

'What sort of car? Can you remember?'

'An old Trr ... Triumph. A cc ... cream one. Sh ... she said once he never cleaned it.'

'Was your ladder so important? Why the hurry to get it at that unearthly hour? Wouldn't next morning have done?'

'Aw. No. I ... I wasn't going Thursday. It was my mother's funeral.'

'Oh. I'm sorry.' Robeson was sympathetically aware of the pale freckled face and lips that trembled.

'I thought the ladder mmm ... might be in Miss Barclay's way. I mean l ... lying there till Friday.'

'So you brought it home?'

'Aw. No.' He paused, as if the recollection still surprised him. 'It wasn't there.'

Robeson wondered if this could possibly be a yarn. But he reckoned the man was too frightened and gormless to invent anything. His sincerity came through in spite of his obvious tension through being questioned.

'Well, have you reported the theft?'

'Aw. N ... no.'

'Why not?' Robeson contained his natural impatience

with people who seemed too frightened to stick up for themselves and enlist the help of authorities.

'I ... I found it. Fr ... Friday. Early. B ... been chucked over the hedge. In the field. T'other side o' the road.' He shrugged his small shoulders. 'Ss ... same vandals I s'ppose. Broke the church window.'

Fingerprints, Robeson thought; probably loads. He wasn't sure if it was worth involving the experts to catch lager louts for having a lark with a ladder. But the church window ... it wasn't the first time.

'Have you used the ladder since?' He held little hope. Today was Monday. If it had been used through the weekend it must have gathered three working days of paint flakes and dust.

'Aw. I ... I worked over weekend. To make up for l ... lost time, an' while the weather holds.'

Robeson's heart sank. 'You used it then.' It was a statement, not a question.

'Aw. No.' Retter's pale eyes opened wider on recollection. 'Not me short ladder. 'Twas me short ladder they took. I been using me long ladder.'

Robeson looked hard at him. He still wondered if it was worthwhile to get the fingerprint boys involved just to catch village idiots, but it seemed nothing else had been done about them; vandals had been a scourge for ages now whenever boredom took them. As long as there was apathetic acceptance, the bloody nuisances would go on getting away with it.

'I presume you keep the ladder on top of the van. Where do you keep the van?'

'Aw. Outside. I haven't got a garage.'

'I'd like you not to touch the short ladder again, Mr Retter. I want to get our fingerprint boys onto it right away.' He saw Ginger's face turn ashen, his freckles stand out. He saw the terror in the bright pale eyes. 'Don't worry. Though they might want your dabs, too.' He felt sorry for the man sitting opposite, looking so ill; his accounts had fitted with others but the ordeal of being questioned was upsetting him badly.

92

'You needn't worry. Your dabs are only needed to eliminate them from any that shouldn't be there; they'll be destroyed.' He waited a moment for his assurance to sink in before going on.

'Now, about this young girl who's missing. Working for Miss Barclay, you saw her. How did they seem to get on?'

'Aw.' Ginger shifted on his chair, it scraped the vinyl-covered floor. 'Aw. All right. I think.'

'Didn't you tell a mate or someone they had a bit of a barney? In fact I believe you said they were at each other's throats?'

'Aw.'

Robeson saw the pale face tinge. He waited.

'Th ... they had a ff ... just a few words p'raps. Mmm ... Miss Barclay ss ... said it were just teenage...'

Robeson accepted that Retter had made certain unguarded remarks. They had probably grown out of proportion each time they were repeated and intoned differently. He thanked him for his help, stood up, and ducked as his head nearly touched the whitewashed ceiling. He would get onto the fingerprint blokes at once. As for helping the police with enquiries...

He was always telling his subordinates never to accept the obvious. But he trusted his own gut feeling that Gordon Anthony Retter was as innocent as he was gormless. He might even have lied in his teeth thinking he was saving that girl Barclay, and why for goodness sake? But whatever had happened to Kim Croft, he wouldn't have had anything to do with it. He was the sort of person to step out of line in a bus queue, and said 'sorry' when others bumped into him.

Except for a remote chance to catch up with some lager louts, the interview had been a waste of time.

10

It wasn't far to walk back to the Incident Room. Apart from getting on to the forensic bureau at Headquarters to deal with Retter's ladder, Robeson was already thinking of what he had to do next.

He knew all about calling on bereaved parents. Circumstances differed but the task didn't get easier, he was glad to be taking Inspector Starks. She irritated him at times by her silences, the fathomless look in those brown eyes that made him wonder just what went on in that head of glossy, boyishly-short fair hair, but he acknowledged her quiet efficiency, if only to himself. She knew exactly when and how to show compassion. She was sensitive to unshed tears, stiffened lips, and the tensing of face muscles. And although his own years of experience had taught him to keep emotionally detached if he were to stay sane, certain duties still moved him deeply. He felt that meeting the parents of the man found hanging from a tree his morning, might be one of them.

He understood they lived at the opposite end of the village. After a brief appearance in the Incident Room to give a few orders, he took one of the Sierras parked outside, and Inspector Starks slid into the passenger seat beside him.

He drove slowly through the long straggling village, looking for 43 High Street. Though why it was called High Street he couldn't imagine. It was the only street. Admittedly there was an inlet here and there where cottages faced each other across cobbled courtyards. He saw an iron pump in the centre of one, actually being used. It crossed his mind there were diehards here still unaware that even Drayford had crawled into the twentieth century with the advent of mains water.

He passed the church. It stood well back from the line of buildings on each side of it, providing a rough square of parking space outside the lych gate. Next, jutting out, was The King's Arms public house, its narrow forecourt decked with beer-barrel tubs filled with begonias, and some rustic tables and forms. He said:

'I take it you know something about these people, Mary?' He'd seen her talking to John Moore before they left, and she always did her homework.

She was peering into her neat shoulder bag checking her notebook and pens and everything she might need was in order. 'They are elderly, apparently. Married late in life. The boy's mother was in her forties when he was born.'

'Good grief!' The tragedy sounded even worse, if that was possible. A mother's only son. Robeson drove on, past the bakehouse that exuded a warm yeasty smell beside its tiny adjoining shop. The Drayford Family Stores was all but hidden by a poster-covered window; promotions and special offers that no doubt vied to compete with the big shops in Draymouth just a short bus ride away. Several hundred yards further on, beyond a field of grazing Friesians, the road was bordered on each side by a terrace of small red brick houses.

Mary pointed. 'There's number forty-three.'

It was on their right, the side of the road where the scanty brook trickled over weeds and watercress beneath little cement bridges. Robeson had half expected to see some sign of activity around the house. Curious bystanders perhaps, or the door open to friends and neighbours going in and out to help another in trouble. A death, especially an untimely end that was not in the natural order of things, always provided its own curious stimulus for those who neither mourned nor were emotionally involved.

But the door of number 43, painted a drab brown, was shut. In the closed sash-window beside it, between dingy lace curtains, stood a potted fern.

He supposed he was glad the house hadn't attracted gawpers, though he guessed curtains would probably be twitched now that his car was parked outside. It would be devastating enough having to witness and console a heartbroken mother, and to find out if her son had left a note indicating his intention to take his own life, without having to detect if there was any link between the boy's death and the missing schoolgirl, Kim Croft.

He tapped at the door with the flap of the letterbox, stiff and rough with corrosion, but the only means available. It was opened after a moment or two by a small balding man with a drooping white moustache stained brown in the middle. Robeson said: 'Mr Pym ... Mr Walter Pym?'

Without answering, the man turned away and called into the dimness behind him, 'Mother?'

Robeson thought idly that the wallpaper, mauve chrysanthemums on a dreary background, probably made the hallway appear smaller than it was.

A tall woman loomed towards the light thrown in from the open door. Her expression and bearing, head-up-shoulders-back, reminded him of pictures he'd seen of a prison wardress with suffragettes. Her flowered pinafore tied round her broad hips did little to alter the image, nor the long brown skirt that nearly reached her ankles. She pushed the small man aside, pressing him against the wall as she filled the open doorway and asked: 'What do you want?'

Robeson looked from one to the other. 'Mr and Mrs Walter Pym?'

'Of course,' she answered for both of them.

'I'm Chief Inspector Howard Robeson, CID. This is Inspector Mary Starks.'

The look she gave them could have splattered insects. Perhaps it was the grief, a defence mechanism, people showed it in different ways. He said: 'I'm very sorry, Mrs Pym. I would like to have let you know we were coming, had you been on the phone.'

'Should I be?' the woman sniffed.

96

It was not a sniff from weeping, thought Robeson, dismayed by the thin mouth, sharp nose, and eyes as lively as a dead cod's on a fishmonger's slab. He said: 'We are extremely sorry to have to bother you at a time like this, Mrs Pym. I'm sure you'll understand it's necessary.' He felt conspicuous standing on the narrow slate step. 'I won't keep you long. There are just a few questions. Do you feel able?'

'Better come in then, I suppose. Wipe your feet.' She paused at the first of two doors and looked down at their shoes. 'In the front room, I suppose.'

Robeson glanced at Inspector Starks. The tiny square room smelt shut in. Musty, mouldy, and damp. Maidenhair flourished in clay pots on the window sill and obscured the light. Bushy ferns shaped like the Prince of Wales plumes stood in pots on Victorian whatnots. More ferns were arranged on the layered shelves of a dark old-fashioned overmantle with a spotted mirror. And pots of damp-looking soil stood on the black-leaded hearth in front of an open fireplace laid with sticks and newspaper.

There was an uneasy moment. Robeson wondered how you offered condolence to someone who showed no sign of grief, and gave the impression any such attempt would be unwelcome. Though he had a gut feeling that the old man was broken. He had heard it in the high trembling call to her, seen it in the bright moist eyes, and the way the forlorn figure in crumpled grey trousers and brown woolly cardigan had shambled in to stand beside Mary. He said: 'Mr and Mrs Pym, you know how extremely sorry...' He wanted to apologise and explain kindly that when these things happen, the police are sometimes obliged to intrude on grief. She stopped him with a flick of her bony hand, and a sucking of teeth.

'Yes, I know all about that, thank you. It's a pretty fine to-do, isn't it? And my people always been respectable.'

Robeson couldn't see the connection. His police-trained eyes noted the hard-looking three-piece suite covered with cold blue damask, the dreary rose-papered walls, pictures of *The Last Supper, The Resurrection of Christ,* and Scripture texts in cheap frames. He would have understood better had the room been a mess with evidence of endless cups of fortifying tea.

She folded her arms. They hid the gaping buttons of her white blouse, taut over a large bust that drooped to waist level, like a cushion with the filling sunk to one end. With a curl of her thin lips, she said: '*We're* Church. *My* people.'

The emphasised *my* people, followed by a glance at her husband, implied that his people didn't share such high standing. She said: 'You'd better sit down, I suppose. But not in that chair.' She indicated the one with an anti-macassar embroidered with *God is Love.* 'I keep that for His Reverence.'

Robeson had no wish to take the seat reserved for the Holy posterior. He preferred, in the unusual circumstances and atmosphere, to remain standing. The seats looked uncomfortable anyway, probably over-stuffed with horsehair. If condolences weren't needed, they might as well get on to other matters. He said, 'Mr and Mrs Pym, do you mind if I ask one or two things?'

'Please yourself then,' she said, drawing herself up. He realised she referred to their not accepting her invitation to sit down. Without answering his question, she went on: 'I understand I can't have the funeral until coroner says. After the inquest. All very fine for him.' She sucked in her teeth. 'How will I know when to get ham in special?' She saw Robeson look at Mary and snapped in her direction: 'And who exactly are you?'

Mary smiled. 'I...' she began and was interrupted.

'I don't hold with women policemen. Where's your uniform? I suppose you're like the postmen these days. They wear any old thing.' She sucked her teeth. 'No wonder dogs go for them. Look like tramps some of them.'

Robeson detected neither heartbreak nor regret, and marvelled how this person could ever have once conceived; how any man could ever have loved her, given her a child?

He looked from one to the other. 'Can you tell me if your son left any kind of note?'

'No!' She answered for both.

'Have you looked? Perhaps in a drawer or a pocket?'

'There's nothing.'

'Have you searched his clothes?' Robeson from his height of six foot saw Mr Pym's fringe of white hair around his speckled head, and asked him specifically. 'Are you sure there's nothing?'

'He wouldn't know,' his wife answered. 'Anyway, what have you people done with William's jacket? William had a jacket.'

'What do you mean?' Robeson asked.

'Your people took me to the mortuary. Minute I saw William there I thought, where's his jacket?'

'It's at the church I expect, Mother.' The old man's voice broke, but choking he managed to say: 'You know he often left it.'

She ignored him and addressed Robeson. 'You leave his jacket be. I'll fetch it back when I go. You won't find anything in there.'

'A note. Or anything might help the inquest, Mrs Pym. How can you be so sure?'

'Because I brushed it out nigh every day, that's why. That jacket cost fifteen pounds ninety-nine at Marks and Spencer's.' She drew her lips back against her teeth as if she were sucking a lemon. 'I didn't pay fifteen pounds ninety-nine for him to stuff the pockets.'

He met her glare as she drew in her face level with the dewlap beneath her receding chin. She reminded him of a short-necked pelican. He said: 'It really would help us, and you, if we found something.'

'Look if you like. But leave it be. You won't find anything.'

Mr Pym passed the back of his hand over his stained moustache and sniffed. 'There are his books, Mother.' He turned to Mary. 'My boy ... my boy's ...' He reached for his handkerchief and buried his face in it. His shoulders shook.

99

'Quiet, Walter.'

'What books, Mr Pym?' Robeson asked kindly.

'My boy ... my boy ... he does write things.' Pym blew his nose. 'He did...'

His wife glowered. 'Talks rubbish, he does.'

The old man wiped his eyes, and his voice broke as he said, 'I've seen. You've never...'

Robeson didn't miss the small heave of the old shoulders and Mary's arm reach out to him; not the straight arm that one lends to comfort a stranger, but curved ready to encircle with warmth and feeling.

'Leave go of him. Outside, Walter! Thinks he can answer back because someone's here.'

He shuffled towards the door like a whipped dog to its kennel, Mary supporting him.

'He doesn't need you. He's going out the back garden. I let him smoke his filthy old pipe out there in the lavatory.'

Mary took no notice. The man broke down in sobs. When they were outside the door, Robeson heard the rising howls of anguish, heaving intakes of breath, and moans of distress. He thanked God Mary was so capable to deal with what sounded like a case of mounting hysteria; an old man pushed to his limits by the death of his boy. And over the brink by his own living Hell.

Mrs Pym glowered after them. If she felt the least uncomfortable about her husband's reaction in front of them, it only showed in a flush of her flabby cheeks and the twitch of her tight mouth. She held her head high, pressing back her weak chin so that her face and neck looked all of a piece. Robeson noted with mounting distaste the badly cut dead straight hair that ended level with the lobes of her ears. He said:

'Mrs Pym, can you tell me where your son was on Wednesday evening, the thirty-first of July?'

'They've got all that. Those policemen that came round. Wasted my time. I was making a cake.'

Robeson could see she wasn't going to enlarge on the statements they did already have in the files. He said: 'Did your son ever mention whether he had met the young girl, Kim Croft?'

She coloured and drew herself up. 'He most certainly did not. He never had any truck with girls. I forbade it.'

Robeson looked round the room; at the only apparent reading matter, a big black Bible on His Reverence's chair, and the antimacassars embroidered with *God is Love*.

The woman went on: 'As the good book says, I taught my son to renounce the devil and all his works.' She raised her eyes glazed and expressionless to the ceiling, and recited: 'The pomps and vanity of this wicked world, and all the sinful lusts of the flesh.'

She looks so smug, thought Robeson. He had been a policeman too long to be easily shocked, but the hypocrisy and coldness in this house had nothing to do with sticks and paper in the grate that were never lit. My God, why do I feel so deeply for a boy I didn't even know? He said: 'But your William was young.'

As if to stop him from what she thought he might be going to say, she countered with: 'And didn't Peter say "Abstain from fleshly lusts, which war against the soul"?'

'Mrs Pym, did your son ever say anything about the girl reported missing?'

'No. Why should he? He took his own life because it must have been our dear Lord's will. But William didn't kill that girl.'

'Who said she's been killed, Mrs Pym?'

'Everyone. Down the baker's. In the Post Office. Missing, then. They're usually found done in, aren't they?' She drew up her shoulders and stuck out her chest. 'William knew nothing about her. He never looked at young hussies. I forbade it.'

Robeson glanced round the room. A room full of nothing: no teacups, no warmth, no tears, no soul. No need for starched antimacassars to protect the chairs and lumpy sofa, for obviously neither hands nor heads were ever allowed to rest against them.

'Mrs Pym, can you remember what time your son came home on the evening of Wednesday, the thirty-first of July?'

'No I can't.'

'He was seen running past The King's Arms, and the baker's, and apparently on up the village in this direction about ten. Does that help?'

'He had to be in by a quarter past. Or I lock that door.'

'Did any of our men come to ask him about it?'

'Yes. Deceitful. I caught one leaving. I'd been down the shop. But William had satisfied him.'

'Well, did your son tell you why he was running home at that time? Seems he had fifteen minutes before he would have been locked out.'

She pursed her lips. There was a pause. Robeson waited. After a few seconds she said: 'No. Not a crime for a young man to run, is it?'

'Of course not. And I'm very sorry to be asking you these things,' he said as kindly as he could. The woman was facing him stony-faced, arms akimbo, in her Sunday room where words of God graced the walls, dank ferns flourished, and sticks in the grate wouldn't be lit till Christmas. He saw it all with angry eyes; a place a young man had escaped from. He said:

'Perhaps if you should recall anything that might help, you could call in the Incident Room. Or ring us.'

'I won't pay for one of those telephone contraptions. D'you know how much they cost?' She glared as if he had personally insulted her to suggest such a thing. 'I use next door's if ever I want.' She sniffed. 'But they're not very friendly. No one is round here.' She glanced at the chair she kept for His Reverence. 'They're not Church.'

Robeson imagined His Reverence was her only visitor; he could sit there, droning in his special Sunday voice, and she would feel good. He moved towards the door, and said: 'Can we see if Mr Pym is feeling better?' But at that moment, Mary came in.

'Mr Pym's all right now,' she said. 'I left him smoking his pipe.'

102

'In the garden I hope. In the lavatory.'

'Yes, Mrs Pym.' Mary glanced at Robeson. He had already decided there was no point in staying, the boy it seemed had left no letter. He thanked Mrs Pym for her help and uttered brief condolences, this time only as a matter of form.

It crossed his mind that William Pym had at least *seen* the girl, Kim Croft, even if his mother didn't know. The information was recorded on statements in the files. He remembered snippets he'd read and heard. The locals' nickname for William Pym was Bible Billy. Some lads had seen the girl follow him out of The King's Arms on that Wednesday evening, and catch him up, around twenty past nine. That was the last time, so far recorded, she was seen by anyone. But apparently William John Pym hadn't told his mother. And Robeson wouldn't have blamed him if he'd never told her anything. Unless it was to go to Hell.

In the car he and Mary exchanged bewildered glances. He sensed they were being watched, that somewhere behind lace curtains in those other houses were people who were human; curious, and sad, but afraid or unable to offer comfort. As police officers, he and Mary were used to seeing apprehension, suspicion, dislike, and sorrow. But for a moment they were at a loss. Mrs Pym had been a new experience. Now it was as if they had escaped into fresh air to catch their breath.

Robeson drove away slowly. He silently admired Mary for the way she showed compassion. Where the road widened at a gateway into a field, he turned the car round. 'Better go and have a quick look at that jacket, I suppose.'

Mary remained silent a moment before she said: 'If I had a mother like that I'd have left home, or committed suicide long before I was twenty.'

He glanced sideways, surprised. The madonna-like calmness she always kept in the face of trauma, and the steadiness in her brown eyes, appeared the same. But her voice, usually full of kindness and understanding, came through gritted teeth and was filled with indignation. He felt the same. He said: 'People have done it for less. Poor sod.'

Five minutes later they were at the church of St John in the Wilderness. Robeson tried the latch of the heavy iron-patterned door. It was locked, but they had no reason to go in. They glanced at notices pinned in the porch; out of date were the Flower Festival, the Meeting of the Mothers' Union, and A Pilgrimage to Glastonbury. Names and addresses of various vicars that served this parish were protected in a small glass case. On a nail in the wall, to their right as they'd come in, hung a man's stone-coloured jacket. Robeson took it down carefully and read the label. St Michael, 67% Terylene. The price, £15.99, was still attached with a short plastic thread. There was no note in any of the pockets, just oddments, and a door key attached to a large wooden tag. Little wonder, thought Robeson, that its owner had apparently often taken the coat off, he would have been terrified to do anything in it that might make it dirty and incur the wrath of his mother. Robeson put it back exactly as he'd found it.

He figured their next call would be the last for the day. The riding school was a couple of miles from the church, but he guessed the area would have attracted attention. Coming from that direction were groups of people whose curiosity had been aroused after the mortuary van, black and sinister, had been reported going up Bridle Lane earlier, and returning. They wouldn't have seen much for their trouble. The large wooden gate, off its hinges and weed-embedded, at the entrance to the old deserted rectory, was sealed off by yards of white tape. A uniformed officer stood guard. He acknowledged the Inspectors with a salute and a smile as they drove by.

Robeson respected his Chief's method of working when he was running a show. There was no better detective at Divisional Headquarters of the CID than Superintendent John Moore. Robeson shared Moore's meticulous attention to detail, an insistence that everything that happened or

104

was reported in the department must be confirmed and cross-checked, over and over.

At the riding school, the proprietor, Miss Knowle, was in the stable. As she rubbed down a magnificent chestnut hunter, she blamed the upsetting events of the day for making her work beyond her usual schedule. She recounted the drama between deep intakes of breath, in a voice which in Robeson's book was distinctly upper-crust: 'It was little Alexander. De ... ar da ... harling Alexander Ponsonby. He saw it. Well, something. His hack was in front. Too far, I do like them to keep together, in line. To wait.' She pushed her hair back out of her eyes; it reminded Robeson of the cottage loaf of his childhood, pumpkin round and crinkly, with a little poked-in bun perched on the top. She went on: 'He stopped in a gateway. I'm always telling Alexander not to wait there. Jodi, that's his hack, will only...' Her voice trailed away as if exasperated by thoughts of his disobedience. Her plummy voice rose: '*Not there, de ... ar*, I was always saying. They just don't listen. And suddenly I heard him shout "Miss Knowles, Miss Knowles!"' She let out a heavy sigh in recollection. 'Shouting. As if ... oh I don't know ... but shouting ... it sounded so dreadfully common.'

Robeson wished she wouldn't digress. It had been a long day. She was a short, thick woman of indeterminate age, with a rosy-apple face. The skin of her hands looked as rough as sandpaper. She probably thought they liked standing on straw, breathing the warm smell of horses as much as she did. But at this point of her account, she patted the fine animal she was rubbing down, turned and faced them.

'Really officer! I hastened to see what was the matter and I couldn't believe my eyes!' She clutched her plump stomach with both hands, opened her mouth and bent her head over to demonstrate her nausea. 'It was in the drive. Just round from the gateway. In a tree. Like washing hung up to dry.'

They waited for her to recover herself. They knew these facts but were getting them first hand. Robeson liked that.

105

She said: 'It was the white shirt. That's what showed up, I suppose.' She paused, and Robeson saw tiny beads of sweat on the suspicion of a moustache that shadowed her upper lip. He waited. After a few seconds she began again, this time pouring out the details that had simultaneously impressed themselves on her mind: 'I saw the face. The mouth open, fixed in a gape. It looked strange. Half smiling. But it could have been scorn.' She paused again. 'I was completely shocked. To see his hands. Hanging there. Such long pale fingers. Beautifully shaped and delicate like a girl's.'

Miss Knowles, almost with a jerk, stopped torturing herself with the memory. She pulled herself together as she must have done this morning and, in her more resolute teacher's voice, she said: 'In a flash I'd got those children back here and sent home, and had phoned Drayford Police House.'

'Now the day is over,' Robeson sang tunelessly as he drove back towards the village. 'I hope,' he added, thinking of an evening at home with Janet, and sparing a thought for John Moore's lot since his wife left him for a man whose job didn't keep him working all hours.

He glanced sideways at Mary; elegantly informal in her white blouse, slim skirt and long dark jacket. He wondered what she must look like, dressed-up, and checked himself, mindful he was happily married. He said: 'And what have we achieved today, Mary?' He let her name slip often when they were working together. He answered his own question. 'Damn all, seems to me, except discover why some poor sod thought he would be better off dead.'

They drew up outside the Incident Room. Mary had left her own car there to drive home to town after they had made their report. Opening her neat shoulder bag, she said: 'There is this, sir.' Like a rabbit from a hat, she produced a red loose-leaf exercise book. 'He wants it back. The old man. It's all he's got. His boy's. I promised.'

Robeson took it. The neat hand-writings looked like the ramblings of a religious maniac.

106

Mary said: 'I thought we, or the Super, might read something into it.' Seeing the look on his face, she added: 'It's a diary. Of a sort.'

He glanced over a page. He recognised the possibility of Mary's feminine intuition. Beneath that stylish fair hair there was a shrewd brain that had proved itself on several occasions before, and earned her promotion. But he felt doubtful as he read: 'July 30th. Silly women laden with sin, led away by divers lusts. Timothy 2. Hebrew Bible. 3.6.

July 31st. It was in my mouth sweet as honey: and as soon as I had eaten it, my belly was bitter. Revelation. 10. 10.

Aug. 1st. Acts Apostles. St Luke. God be merciful to me a sinner. 13.

For this thing was not done in a corner. 26.'

His glance scanned down the page to the last entry:

'Aug. 4th. The Epistle of Paul to the Romans: 6. 23. The wages of sin is death.'

11

Death was on Raine's mind. There seemed no chance to forget when it was reported in the local paper, on radio, and television. She tormented herself, why had Bible Billy, that fine-looking boy, taken his life? He had apparently gone about his normal business for the past six days, so his death could have nothing to do with Kim's disappearance.

She moved around the house; arranged flowers, adjusted folds in the curtains, and prayed: please God, no more questions. Questions questions questions. That wretched Inspector Robeson had come three times yesterday. She was coming to dislike his well-spoken, kind-fatherly way of extracting information from her that she had thought irrelevant. He was a curly-headed monster with dark eyes that didn't miss a blink. His very presence made her feel exposed; every buried thought, unsafe. The tone of his questions, put with such apparent kindness and understanding at first, had turned quite nasty when she told him she had sold her car. She hadn't mentioned it before because she'd thought, why involve a complete stranger who by chance had seen her advertisement, bought the car, and just happened to choose to collect it on Wednesday? It had nothing to do with Kim.

In the drawing room she moved a piece of Capo di Monte, appreciating the exquisite craftsmanship; an old man on a rustic seat. She admired the intricate detail, a robin perched on the toe of his boot. Then she decided the ornament looked better standing where it was before. She put it back on the small table next to the crystal bowl of yellow roses. She needed to be doing something; touching, rearranging, putting things in line, anything to help her forget. But thoughts of death flowed back with the persistence of flood water under a door.

This latest happening in the village was reported yesterday. Today there were comments, conjectures, remarks that it might not be a coincidence, happening so soon after Kim's disappearance. She swallowed hard. Was it going to provoke more questions? She looked from the drawing-room window without seeing the wide common and the distant sea, but remembering Inspector Robeson and his assistant standing like grand inquisitors in the middle of the room. She had stated when asked, that Kim had made no friends or acquaintances here. How would that Robeson man react this time if now she were to admit that Kim had met a boy called William? But why should she tell him? She only had Kim's word for it. Kim's alleged meeting, her adolescent boasting that she was the first girl that William had ever kissed, was more than likely not true. To repeat her lies might cause unnecessary complication, and she could certainly do without that, especially now Monica was coming.

It seemed to Raine that her own mind could only take so much. One wrong word from Monica, Jeffrey, or anybody, and her pent-up feelings might spill over into some kind of physical outpouring that she couldn't control.

She went into the kitchen. There was the evening meal to plan for three. She wondered if she would be able to cope with what would be Monica's natural grief and anxiety. Over the past week she had made herself pot after pot of strong tea as she brooded on all the awful implications, the mental stripping and looks of suspicion cast her way.

But she hoped that was over now. She thought: Outside this body of mine, this torment, life is going on. I must get on with it. Survive. I must. I must think of Monica. And however distraught and difficult Monica might be to console, her company while Jeffrey was in his Draymouth office all day would at least detract from the charged emptiness, the deadly silence of the house. At this moment all

109

she could hear was the small movement outside as Ginger went about his painting. She wondered what went on in his sad mind now? She spoke to him only when necessary. She felt mean to see him produce his own vacuum flask at mid-morning and squat down by the rockery to drink. But she couldn't face asking him into the kitchen, too many questions hung in the air.

Yet the quietness in the house was filled with her self-incrimination. She felt a stab of guilt, sharp as the blade of a flick knife. Suppose that shy, handsome boy they called Bible Billy, really had taken to Kim, and been upset by her disappearance?

It was mid-afternoon when Raine heard a car. She reached the front door in time to see it being driven away, and a well-remembered figure standing on the step. Monica's blue eyes were almond-shaped like Kim's, and her short hair with its natural wave, a lighter shade of demerara.

Raine threw her arms around her in a hug of silent sympathy, ready to deal with tears. But apart from a slight sniff and a handkerchief pressed to her upper lip, Monica appeared composed.

Raine looked for a bag or something to carry in. 'Didn't you bring anything ... I mean ... a case?'

Monica's mouth fell open. 'Oh. My dear Raine, I'm sorry. Were you expecting me to stay? Oh dear. I *am* sorry. Have I put you out?'

'Oh no. Not at all.' Raine had taken staying for granted. Jeffrey had said Monica phoned, was coming down, together they would go to the Incident Room to find out how enquiries were going.

She led the way to the drawing room.

Monica explained: 'Andy, my boyfriend, brought me down. He's going to pick me up later. Take me to Draymouth for dinner.' She put her head on one side. 'You don't mind, do you?'

'Of course not.' Raine recognised the same gesture that Kim used on occasions in abortive efforts to look sensual and appealing.

'We found a lovely little hotel. Right on the seafront.' Monica curled herself into an armchair. 'You'll have had enough of me by six. And Jeffrey will be home. It's hardly the thing, is it? I mean ... me and my ex in the same house.'

Over a cup of tea Raine recounted events. Then the massive hunt, the army of mounted police drafted from up-country, men on foot with tracker dogs combing the common, helicopters throbbing overhead from dawn till God knows when, and the co-operation of the public. During the weekend they had raked fields, searched hedges, scanned ditches, and dragged ponds.

'All for my sweet little Kim.' Monica looked plaintive. 'We are like sisters. I told those plain-clothes men when they came. I gave her everything she ever wanted. I let her do her own thing. My sweet little sister.'

Raine couldn't dismiss an age gap of twenty-six years so easily. And where, she wondered, was Monica's dress sense? Her full skirt was short and provocative enough to make men wonder what was underneath. Raine felt, after listening for an hour to sexist patter, that if Monica were alone with a man it wouldn't be long before she let him find out.

'More tea?' Raine asked.

'Oh please. Thank you.' Monica handed over her cup. 'Andy's been absolutely wonderful. Taking time off. Bringing me down. Not everyone would.' She rearranged herself on the chair in an unsuccessful attempt to cover her thighs. 'He's an absolute darling. But you, my dear Raine ... Jeffrey told me just what you've had to put up with. And it's not as if it was your fault.'

Raine took momentary relief from her attitude, and poured them both more tea. 'I think what got the police steamed up was we didn't report that Kim was missing until we felt sure. They didn't seem to believe us when we said she sometimes stayed out late.'

'Silly pigs. I never kept my sweet little Kim in a miserable straitjacket. Every little individual should express their own personality.'

Raine recalled her first impression of Monica when they

111

had met two years before; pretty in a baby-doll way, but smooth and crisp like a meringue with not much inside. She said: 'Jeffrey was going to find a boarding school.'

'Boarding school?' Monica's short laugh sounded derisive. 'My sweet little Kim just wouldn't stay in one. And I wouldn't let her. Those places stifle their little egos. She left two boarding schools.'

Raine recalled seeing the word *expelled* on the tabloids. She said: 'Jeffrey said he would.'

'My dear Raine, you don't know him like I do. He's got no idea. I brought her up. I gave her everything.' She sipped her tea, then added with a short laugh: 'Like a big sister.'

Raine didn't answer. She reflected idly that Monica had passed no remark about the view; most people did when they came to the house for the first time; called it 'out of this world'. No doubt she preferred skylines of rooftops, casinos, and high-rise blocks. As for conversation, she spoke only of men, and Kim, in that order. The former brought a glow to her fair skin, light into her blue eyes. She controlled her animation when it was Kim's turn. Raine detected the change of tone didn't come naturally, but as a result of irritation, like having to apply brakes in the midst of a joyride.

With a marked switch to her serious voice, Monica said: 'My sweet little Kim. I wonder what she would like for Christmas. When she comes back.'

Raine glanced over the rim of her cup. It was only August. Did Monica believe...? Was she really optimistic, or was this an act to obliterate the need to face other possible facts?

Monica went on: 'But I must say she's being very naughty. Heaven knows why she went off this time. Jeffrey doesn't know. You don't know. I don't know.' Monica finished her tea and put down her cup. 'She had everything she wanted. I saw to that. She's never stayed away this long before.' Monica shrugged, and sounded as if she preferred to dismiss the subject. 'Andy says I shouldn't worry. I don't need that kind of stress. It'll do me no good. He really is a pet. He's been marvellous. But you can't help worrying, can you, when you're like a big sister?'

Raine tightened her lips. Facing her was a divorcee of forty, in an unsuitable diaphanous dress; designed, one suspected, for the benefit of men, Andy in particular. With Monica's every intake of breath and practised heave, she revealed her voluptuous breasts unfettered by a bra. Raine wanted to shout: *You are not her sister! You are her mother! You are ten years older than I am!* Instead she thought, God! If only I'd known. I should have made more effort. Befriended Kim. I did try, but I gave up, let my patience snap.

She felt guilty. More guilt than she had endured this past seven days. Kim had obviously never known real love. But following example, had found warmth in men's arms; enjoyed flattery, kisses, and cuddles. They probably helped serve the need, as much as gifts and bribes did, to keep out of Monica's way. Even more than a Sony radio cassette.

Raine thought, there's nothing else to do, I must be polite, sit here and listen. But her eyes glazed as Monica chatted, animated and almost without pause, about the big hunky men who'd called on her in London to make enquiries. Really lovely men they were, quite divine one of them was. Monica had told those adorable chaps it was important to let children stay free, do their own thing; self-expression did sometimes cause little setbacks, the odd row at times, but it prepared them for life, didn't it? And anyway, discipline was an ugly word in her book.

Raine picked up a white speck from the carpet. She looked forward to Jeffrey's coming home. More especially she could hardly wait for six o'clock and Andy's arrival; not because Monica assured her she would find him simply gorgeous when she met him, but she hoped he would, without too much delay, take Monica back to their hotel in Draymouth.

No doubt, Raine reflected, when Jeffrey took Monica to the village hall tomorrow to enquire as to the progress of the search, Monica, if not too dazzled by the police officers, would rise to the occasion, act the caring mother and use her special, lowered voice. If there was nothing doing, perhaps she would hang around the area a couple of days more for decency's sake, popping in for a chat and coffee, before escaping back to London with Andy.

Raine was not entirely right. After Monica's visit with Jeffrey to the police Incident Room, and a cursory look at the village and surroundings, she went home later the same day. She was obviously relieved to have been told there was no reason for her to stay around Drayford unless she wished to. For the moment, there was nothing more she could do to help the police.

Though there had been no progress to report to Kim's parents, the Incident Room still buzzed. Lording over yet another Press conference was Superintendent John Moore, a man whose head looked large in proportion to his small eyes. He barked: 'Don't forget the further description of Kim Croft. Yes, again. Inspector Robeson has learnt she was probably carrying a Sony radio cassette. If anyone's seen this girl, or finds the Sony. You know the rest. Phone this number, or Draymouth, or any police station.' He narrowed his little eyes. There were so many lines to follow, but he knew when and who to delegate.

With the Press conference out of the way, he was glad to see PC Trevor Drew had joined them from the local police house. And Detective Sergeant Roger Mills was at his desk. Roger had served his two years as a uniformed officer here in Drayford before being sent elsewhere. Eventually promoted, he had come back to the Force in Draymouth. Moore called: 'Roger. And you, Trevor. Reckon you two should know more than anyone about the people in this place. What's the latest earful? Anything off the record from the landlord of The King's Arms?'

Drew said: 'Nothing new, sir. He doesn't even remember the girl. So he says. But he would, wouldn't he, she was under age.'

Mills put in: 'His excuse is his place gets packed.

114

Especially August. Visitors. He never saw her. Nor did his assistant. Funny everyone else did.'

It had already been well-documented that Kim followed Bible Billy out of The King's Arms around twenty past nine on Wednesday, 31st July. A gang of youths skylarking outside at the time had been further witness. Everyone knew everyone in the village and a stranger was obvious.

Moore said: 'What of William Pym? Was he a regular in there?'

'Oh yes, sir.' Drew was glad of a chance to air his local knowledge. 'Used to keep to himself at the end of the bar. Sipping a lemonade shandy. Never stayed more than twenty minutes.' Drew paused to consider what next might be of use. He'd picked up a lot of extraneous information, trained as they all were to be forever listening whether on duty or not, and to use the third eye in the back of their heads. He went on: 'Then he'd go round to the church. Not to pray. Least I don't think so. It was God's house. He guarded it. Not God. Pym I mean. He told someone.'

Mills quipped: 'He couldn't do much else on the strength of a lemonade shandy.'

Moore scowled but smiled inside, the light edge sometimes kept one sane. He said: 'Around ten to ten, Pym was seen on his own, going up the village towards his home. Some said running, some said walking. Apparently when questioned he gave the DC a perfectly satisfactory explanation.' Moore tapped his fingers on the table. 'But that was on Wednesday, Trevor. What was Pym doing on Thursday and Friday, in fact every day until his body was found on Monday? You must've been spreading yourself around even more than usual this past week with your eyes and ears flapping.'

'Yes, sir. Nothing like this has ever happened in the village before. It's on everyone's lips. A nine-days' wonder.'

Mills grinned: 'Looks like being ninety-nine.'

Moore concentrated on Drew. He repeated: 'Do you know how Pym filled his last few days, Trevor? What was he doing?'

115

'Well he couldn't have been doing anything out of the ordinary, sir. Someone would have noticed. Everyone knows about everyone else in the village. He was in church on Sunday. Giving out hymn books, and taking the collection. Then Monday...'

'Can't you account for the other days?'

Drew shook his head. 'He was probably in the churchyard. He was always there. A sort of voluntary odd job boy. The chap that keeps the yard tidy might know more.'

'What's he called?'

'Fred Palmer. Thinks he's Drayford's answer to Capability Brown. Drop a sweet paper in his churchyard at your peril.'

Mills grinned. 'I remember him. Involved in a bit of juicy gossip once. Years back apparently. Long before I did my stint here.'

'Personal, or relevant, Roger?' Moore asked.

'Irrelevant, sir, sorry. I was just reminded.'

Moore glanced at Drew. 'Have you heard, Trevor?'

The constable shook his head, and Moore turned back to hear the rest from Mills. 'Oh it's probably forgotten at last, sir. It was ancient history even in my time. Only rehashed pub talk. But it came back to me when Trevor mentioned him. That's all. Sorry.'

'Well, we may as well have it,' Moore said. 'We like to know all about people we're going to talk to.' He called across the room to Chief Inspector Robeson: 'Howard. You can go and see this Mr Palmer. Ask if he can throw some light on Pym's last days.' Moore addressed Sergeant Mills again: 'Is he married, Roger?'

'Well that's what all the fuss was about, sir. Real *News of the World* stuff. Only lasted one night.'

'You mean the marriage, I presume.' Moore was a stickler for clarity.

'Next morning... A few words between them and she fell from the hotel balcony.'

'Killed?'

'No. And nothing was proved. Went on record as an accident. She got away with a broken leg. Lucky for him.'

'Then what?' Moore wanted the full picture. Inspector Robeson listened in.

Mills reflected. 'Local girl apparently. Though she never came back to Drayford. And her people moved away.' He paused. 'Palmer lived it down, I suppose. But a chap doesn't like his performance laughed at, does he? Never. And certainly not on his honeymoon, let alone full details splashed across that certain Sunday paper.'

Moore pulled a face. He had a broken marriage, but not on that score. He said: 'So what's the position now, Roger? Did he marry again?'

'He hadn't when I was here. And hardly likely to, sir. Everyone reckoned he was impotent. But Trevor would know more than I do,' he added, looking at Constable Drew.

'Definitely not married,' Drew said. 'He lives in the village with his widowed sister. I took it he'd always lived with her. A bachelor from choice.'

12

Detective Inspector Robeson had hoped to join other members of the County Naturalist Group for the group's bird watch on the Dray Estuary. But yet again he hadn't the time; this morning he was going to have a few words with Fred Palmer about William Pym. This afternoon he and Inspector Starks were off to interrogate Monica Croft's ex-boyfriend, John Watson. That would entail a forty-mile trip. Watson, a commercial traveller, was on record as having threatened the life of Kim Croft after she had falsely accused him of attempted rape. He had been reported seen on the 31st July in Draymouth.

Robeson's first enquiry was nearer home. He walked from the Incident Room to the Church of St John in the Wilderness. He had never been there before, but from all accounts Wilderness was a misnomer. He hoped his visit wouldn't coincide with a wedding, or a funeral, or even a christening; he didn't want to attract people's curiosity. But there was no point in calling at Palmer's home; he understood the man practically lived in his beautifully kept churchyard.

Inside the black oak lych gate, Robeson paused. Old yew trees, their convex sides and flat tops pruned with precision, lined the gravel path to the church door. The grass between the graves was neat, a good colour despite the lack of rain. Wide borders near the path were weed-free, as velvet smooth as a bowling green.

He strolled on, enjoying the morning, listening for birds, but he knew few sang in August. A sparrow perched on the rim of an empty vase. A blackbird, as he approached, swooped across his path like a low-flying aircraft. He noticed, half-screened by a trellis of climbing roses, there stood a wooden rail hung with enamel jugs and polythene containers. Alongside was a standpipe. The tap dripped, sending a little river along the path and under a green bin. On top of the bin was a large notice written in black paint on a piece of board: *Please put all your paper wrappings and dead flowers here, and replace the lid. Thank you. Fred Palmer.*

Good for you, Fred, thought Robeson. The message was obviously heeded. He reckoned he could enjoy himself here if he had the time. It was so quiet, with nothing to disturb the birds that would come from the hedges nearby and disport themselves among the tombs; dip tiny beaks into brimming vases, throw back their heads to let the water down their grateful throats.

Today the sun was less fierce than of late and all the better for that, he thought, admiring the clean, tidy paths. He glanced at granite gravestones with indecipherable inscriptions, their history hidden beneath sun-crisp yellow lichen.

Memorials of marble, Portland stone, and plain wooden crosses, all perfectly aligned, reminded him of war cemeteries he'd seen in France and Belgium. He walked on slowly. A few yards behind the church, a thickset man with a face as round as an Edam cheese, was manoeuvring a pair of long-handled shears. Instinctively Robeson knew this was Palmer.

'Good morning. Mr Palmer?'

'Aye.'

'I'm Chief Inspector Robeson, CID.' He was alert to the effect that his unexpected visits invariably had on people; tensed face muscles, eyes filled with suspicion. 'I was wondering if you could tell me anything about the late William Pym. I believe he spent a lot of time here.'

'Oh aye. 'E did an' all.'

Robeson gauged Palmer to be about fifty; possibly a cider drinker, but his high colour could be from his exposure to all weathers. 'What can you tell me about him?'

'Oh worl ... a bit soft if you'm askin' me. Always ready

119

to say a prayer.' He curled his lips, and Robeson noted the tired, red-rimmed eyes. 'But that don't mean nought, do it? 'E done it, didn't 'e?'

'Done what?'

'Worl ... tis obvious, innit? That girl.'

'How did he seem to behave the five days prior to his death. Anything different? Did he come here every day as usual?'

'Oh aye,' Palmer answered immediately then paused to reconsider. 'Oh no, I tell a lie. 'E weren't 'ere Thursday.'

'Can you be sure about that?'

'Oh aye.'

'What makes you so sure?'

'Worl. I remember 'e weren't 'ere Thursday cos 'twas little Mrs Retter's fun'ral. 'E often come to funerals. An' he never come.'

Robeson waited.

Palmer went on: 'But he come after. I mean t'other days. But you mark my words. He done it all right.'

Robeson didn't care for know-alls, the village was full of them; people who knew the answers before he knew them himself. He surmised Palmer was accustomed to working without a shirt on; his broad chest glistened with sweat, his shoulders were tanned but for a necklace of white skin where he obviously usually wore a neckerchief. Robeson said: 'It's not known that anything's been done, Mr Palmer.'

'Worl ... p'raps not. But 'tis obvious, innit? You can't trust they Bible thumpers.' He broke off and looked down at Robeson's large black shoes. 'D'you mind keeping off they edges, sir.'

Robeson moved his big feet smartly, surprised by the sergeant-major bark.

'Takes a lot of graft to square they edges. Keep 'em neat. 'Tis sacrilege to spoil church garden.' Palmer rested back on the handle of his long shears and took up his attitude of judge again. 'He done it, all right.'

'Done what?'

120

'Worl ... that girl ... that's what you be come about fer cert'in.'

'I wanted to know if Pym ever said anything that would give any indication of how he was thinking, or if he did anything different from usual during his last days?'

'Nah. I can't say 'e did. But deep, that one. You'd never know what was going on inside 'is 'ead.'

'You said "'E done it".'

'Worl ... ev'ry one'll tell thee Bible Billy done it. Why else did 'e tear a sheet in strips an' make a noose for 'iself?'

Robeson didn't answer. He waited for Palmer to go on.

'I bet 'is mother'd make 'im pay fer thickee sheet if 'er cud.' He curled his thin lips. "E proved 'e done it. Why else would 'e 'ave traipsed all up Bridle Lane to the Judas tree?' Palmer wiped his mouth with the back of his hand. "E knowed 'e'd done wrong, that's why, didn't 'e? Like that disciple bloke done, they says. In the Bible.' He gave a short laugh which sounded all the more insensitive in the surroundings.

Robeson felt he was getting only generalisations, a rehash of what was on everyone's lips. He changed his tack: 'I believe vandals broke the church window on the night of Wednesday, the thirty-first of July. Did the vicar, or perhaps the verger, tell you what, or if anything, was stolen?'

'Nah. Nothing was stolen. There's no verger. Not proper. Not since old Charlie Green kicked the bucket 'bout six months ago.'

Robeson watched the red moon face and wondered how much relevant information would be forthcoming, or if he was wasting his time. He prompted: 'And the vicar...?'

"E's a heller to get on with. Reverend Potter. On 'is last legs. Leaves everything to Mothers' Union.' Palmer sniffed his derision. 'An' to anyone else soft enough to do 'is donkey work. Like Bible Billy.'

'What sort of donkey work?'

'Worl. Anything. Everything. Fer a start, 'e never locked up. Lazy bugger. Give me one key.' He paused. 'I never 'ad much need of it. I mostly give it to Billy. If I wanted to be

121

shot of it I'd just put it in 's pocket.' Palmer took out his handkerchief and wiped his neck. ''Is jacket were usually left 'anged up in the porch.'

'How many keys are there?' Robeson asked.

'Only two. Far's I know. Old Green lost one, and that weren't replaced, I don't think.'

Robeson thought a moment. He had already spoken with the ageing vicar, and others, about what had happened at the church, but he was an avid collector of versions. He said: 'This broken window, was it reported?'

'Nah.'

'Why not?'

'They does it fer kicks.'

'Who're they?'

'Vandals. Not local lads. Their trick's to scatter me bin. I'll catch 'em at it one night, just you see if I don't!' He broke off abruptly, picked up a stone and raised his thick hairy arm to hurl the missile across the graves, but instead he dropped it back beside his foot. 'Thought that was a bloody dog. I keeps a stone 'andy. Don't want them in yer doin' their business.'

Robeson drew diverse threads of information together in his mind. 'I understand the window that was broken was plain glass. Bit odd. Austere for a church, wasn't it?'

'Oh aye. But the one before that, that they vandals broke, was irreplaceable. So vicar said. Medieval or summit.'

Robeson knew from official sources all about the priceless window that had been broken beyond repair, and replaced with ordinary glass until funds could be raised to fit something more in keeping with the fifteenth-century church. He said: 'Apparently, these last reputed vandals cleared the plain window right out; not a small shard left. What happened to the glass?'

Palmer studied the ground. He thought a moment. 'Worl ... I cleaned it up, didn' I? Couldn't 'ave it lying round.'

'Was it broken? Or intact? Any blood about? Where did you put it? In your bin?'

'Nah. Broken all right. No room in me bin. I took it 'ome.

It's gone now. Dustcart's been. I did'n want nothing 'ere messing up the place.'

Robeson felt furious with the silly man. 'Didn't it occur to you, Mr Palmer, that the glass would've been covered with fingerprints? And it's an offence to tamper with evidence?'

'Nah. I didn' know nought about that,' Palmer said as if he didn't care. 'You won't never catch 'em.'

'How can you be so sure?'

'' Twasn' big enough.'

'What do you mean? What wasn't?'

'The bloody window.'

'What for?' Robeson pressed.

'Worl ... fer anyone to get in. It looked bigger than 'twas. I expect because the glass were clear.'

Robeson had done his homework. Only the lowest section of a tall window had been broken. 'The aperture is ten by seventeen inches. Perhaps a child ... or slim person?'

'Well, nothing were took,' Palmer snapped.

Robeson noted the man's finality in his retort, his ill-tempered acceptance that the vandals had had no motive other than to cause a nuisance, so the subject might as well be closed. But Robeson asked himself, why had they gone to the trouble to leave no shards to cause injury, and no fingerprints on the window frame or surrounding stonework? He said: 'That happened some time on the evening or night of the thirty-first of July. That same evening Mr Pym was seen going up the village. Some say walking, some say hurrying, one even said Pym was running.' He pushed a lock of his curly hair from his eyes. 'That was apparently about ten to ten. Though some say ten-ish; others a quarter past. You don't think he might have broken the window?'

Palmer's mouth fell open. He looked stunned. Then his laugh, irreligious, without mirth, shattered the peaceful graveyard peace. 'Billy?'

Robeson waited. Palmer seemed to draw into himself, as if the suggestion was something he hadn't considered.

123

Robeson wondered what he was thinking; quick to note the moment Palmer's beefy face brightened, and a light that hadn't been there before, came into the rheumy eyes.

''Course!' Palmer said: 'I 'spect that were it. Billy were upset! He must've seed 'em when 'e were doin' 'is church-yard watch!' Palmer's laugh sounded less sinister, more of relief. He looked squarely at Robeson. 'Aye. That were it. Fer certin. Always on lookout fer vandals were Billy. I often wondered what 'e'd do. Run like bloody 'ell I'd be bound, or they might spoil 'is pretty face. Seems I were right. 'E did run like bloody 'ell.'

'He was a nice-looking boy, then?'

'A bloody pansy.'

'Then what about girlfriends? Did he talk about girls?' Robeson didn't miss Palmer's smirk, the way he twitched awkwardly as if he had an itch between his shoulder blades.

'I dunno nought 'bout they,' Palmer said curtly. ''E were mummy's boy.' He paused, his thin lips curled. 'But when they sort do slip the apron strings...' He drew a black handkerchief from the pocket of his baggy trousers and wiped the sweat from his face and the back of his neck. 'They'm worst of the bloody lot. He done it all right. You mark my words. There'll be proof.'

Robeson wondered in passing if Palmer, who leaned heavily forward again on the long handle of his shears, was himself spoiling the blades, the ground, or his neatly squared edges. He said: 'Mr Palmer, would you call your-self a religious man?' He cast his eyes over the churchyard and knew his admiring glance wasn't lost, yet Palmer's thin lips tightened.

'Nah. I bloody wouldn't. No God ever did nought fer me.' He looked uncomfortable and twisted his shoulders.

Robeson waited.

'Man to man,' Palmer said, lowering his gravelly voice so that Robeson should know he was being told in confidence, 'Nature played me a dirty trick. When I were a young man, that is. But that ain't no one's, bloody business.' He wiped his mouth with the back of his hand. 'It's another story.

Neither 'ere nor yer. Except 'tis the reason you'll never catch me toadying to no bloody wimmin, nor going down on me knees to pray to 'e up there. Not Sundees nor never.'

Robeson nodded, looked sober, and hoped he appeared to understand. He guessed he'd had the details already among the tittle-tattle that drifted his way; and Palmer's reputed impotence, his traumatic marriage, was irrelevant to this case. Robeson knew it sounded lame, but he said kindly: 'So you are not a believer?'

'Not bloody likely. Not in 'e above. My God be me churchyard.' He looked around him and, as if even he might not want to be cut off completely from salvation, he added: 'Anyway, I believe someone said once ... you be nearer to God in a garden than anywhere else.'

Robeson grinned. 'That's right. They did. Or rather, she did. It's in a poem. God's Garden. By Mrs Dorothy Frances Gurney.'

Palmer blinked. 'I don't know 'er.'

'She's dead,' Robeson said, remembering it was the second line that he loved, and how his wife always teased him for using any excuse to talk birds. But Janet wasn't here to chide him; so smiling to himself he recited.

> 'The kiss of the sun for pardon,
> The song of the birds for mirth,
> One is nearer God's heart in a garden
> Than anywhere else on earth.'

Palmer wiped his face again. 'Aye then. This be my garden. I keeps it like no one else. It's mine. I don't let no one mess it.'

Robeson continued to smile. Proximity to birds invariably relaxed him, and did now, as far as it was possible to relax with impressions, facts, and details buzzing in his head, like a jigsaw puzzle scrambling to be put together. He said: 'Well, thank you, Mr Palmer. I'll leave you to get on with your good work. You've been very helpful.'

Robeson made his way back towards the Incident Room

and reclaimed his car that he had left parked outside. Before this afternoon's trip with Inspector Starks to see John Watson, he intended to drive the twelve miles back to Divisional Headquarters and to put in a couple of hours' work in his own office. He wondered just how long before strands of information from the thousands of questionnaires, statements, and inquiry forms that had recently been amassed, came together with a lead to what had really happened to Kim Croft, and to her whereabouts. Would he still be analysing them when the cold weather brought birds from Northern Europe in search of food? When the usual large flocks of Brent geese arrived in the Dray estuary from Siberia?

Today the roads were still busy with summer traffic. During the frustratingly slow drive, Robeson mulled over the progress made so far towards solving his two most recent cases. Forensic had come up with three different sets of fingerprints on William Pym's exercise book; Pym's own, his father's, and Mary Starks's. Mr Retter's ladder had shown clear palm prints, and fingerprints that were neither Pym's nor Retter's. But they matched nothing on file. Robeson swore; why was everything left so clean around the church window? Now, thanks to that stupid Fred Palmer, it was unlikely that even the church vandals would be brought to book.

Robeson seethed, though he supposed he should spare a mite of sympathy. He hadn't missed the bitterness in the man's thin lips; the resentment that like canker in the core of an apple, obviously gnawed and festered in Palmer's little tub body. Was he really too stupid and ignorant to do something practical to alleviate what troubled him? Didn't he know that these days medical help was available? Instead it seemed that his answer to the bitterness he harboured deep within himself, through his sexual inadequacy, was to create a beautiful churchyard; to ensure that everything around him was immaculate. And in his maniacal pursuit of perfection, he had disposed of possible vital evidence.

Robeson drove slowly; there was little else he could do in the traffic congestion. Why, he asked himself, did they have to dig up the roads in August? It took him almost an hour to reach the large square building of Divisional Headquarters on the outskirts of the city, its whitish grey brickwork reminiscent of a giant public convenience. In his own office, decently large on the third floor, he found, in spite of his usual adrenalin-charged enthusiasm for his latest case, the paperwork waiting on his desk looked daunting. But first he analysed his latest interview. Everything that Fred Palmer had said was consistent with that said earlier by the vicar of Drayford, the Reverend Potter.

Robeson went over that previous interview with Potter. The old crow of a man, well past his job, had also said nothing had been stolen from the church on 31st July. Furthermore, there was no evidence of anyone having entered it by the window or by any other way. In the circumstances Potter had decided there seemed no point in involving the police. Robeson had concluded His Reverence was too apathetic to care much about anything.

Robeson reached for a file. On 31st July, according to the Reverend Potter, Mr Pym had locked the church door at around half past nine. That was not unusual. Pym was aware of possible vandalism. He often locked up. He appeared to enjoy the responsibility. On that evening he had been particularly careful to do his voluntary duty, because in the church, lying in a coffin, was the body of a Mrs Anne Retter.

Robeson flicked over the page. His Reverence had explained: *Mrs Retter's cottage where she had lived with her son, is very tiny. And the local undertaker has no Chapel of Rest. In the circumstances...*

Robeson had asked: 'Can you remember who attended the funeral the following day?'

Potter had said: 'I'm afraid I can't. Just the family, I think. Her son, Mr Retter. His married sister, I think. Perhaps a scattering of friends and neighbours.'

Robeson had not placed too much reliance on the thin,

shaky voice. He thanked Potter for his help and said he would come back later if he needed a statement.

Now Robeson closed the file. On reflection it seemed to him that everything Mr Palmer had said today, about the vicar of Drayford, was correct. The man was old, tired, and obviously quite prepared to let other people do much of his work.

It was hardly surprising, thought Robeson, that the medieval church window, smashed ages ago, hadn't yet been replaced with stained glass. To raise sufficient funds the Mothers' Union probably had to cope alone with their sales of work, church bazaars, and jumble sales.

It was always Robeson's fear when working on a case that the trail might go cold. A massive search for Kim Croft was still going on, but he wondered how much longer they would be allowed to keep the borrowed policemen and horses. So far they had found only a cardigan, a handbag, and one running shoe. None was identified by Raine Barclay as having belonged to Kim. And if the flying allegations and rumours that Bible Billy had murdered her were believed, some zeal might have gone from the hunt. His men were looking for a body, but would assume their success wouldn't be followed by a conviction.

His thoughts returned to the church window. It was six feet from the ground. It needed a slim, athletic type to attempt to get in. Or a ladder. William Pym from all accounts was tall and slight. Gordon Anthony Retter was small and wiry; he had the expertise for removing windows. Robeson shook his curly head. That idea was ludicrous. Or had Retter's account of his temporarily stolen ladder been just a yarn to blind him? Robeson discounted the theory almost before it took shape. Retter hadn't even foreseen Forensic would examine his ladder for fingerprints. His surprised reaction to the suggestion, Robeson had accepted as genuine. Retter would not have purposely planted on his ladder someone else's large palm prints.

Robeson's fragmented thoughts excited him, kept him keyed up. He looked forward to his session tomorrow in the Incident Room. He would by then have interrogated John Watson, the man falsely accused of rape. And whatever came out of that, there was always the cut and thrust of opinions, the exchange of ideas, and more snippets that the sleepy public might have remembered and belatedly put forward.

It was evening, after his interview with John Watson, that Robeson returned with Inspector Starks to Drayford. She had left her own car outside the Incident Room. It saddened him to see her drive off to where he knew she lived with her mother. A lovely young woman like her should be married with kids, not devoting her life to the Force, to atone for the loss of her boyfriend two years ago in Northern Ireland. He hoped one day, she would get over her loss.

He put aside thoughts of work, and feelings of sympathy for Mary Starks. It had been a long day. He reckoned he too deserved to go home. Even though he spent little time there, he was well content that he had a good wife and a decent house. So many of his colleagues, like John Moore, had become case-hardened and bitter. But he had Janet to keep him sane. It would be only minutes after he came into the house that there would be a well-cooked meal on the table.

He always tried not to take his work home with him. He relaxed in an easy chair. But tonight his brain still whirled.

Janet said: 'Quiet tonight, aren't we? Dreaming of birds, love?'

He opened his eyes and grinned.

She chided: 'As long as it's only the feathered kind.'

He smiled again. She didn't expect an answer. Actually, if only Janet knew it, and he certainly wouldn't tell her, he was thinking of a rather good-looking young bird called Raine Barclay. Where, if anywhere, he wondered, did she fit in?

13

Raine looked around the dining room and bit her lip. Since Aunt Jo's arrival yesterday, her personal possessions, an old felt hat, dresses, cardigans, even a raincoat, were on the chairs instead of in the wardrobe provided for them in the hall. Spare sandals and sensible shoes she might need for walking littered the floor.

'Lorraine, my darling,' she had said as Raine helped her unpack, 'there's absolutely no need to hide my things away. I like them handy. Then should the weather change I can pop into them just when I want to.' Her small round face, webbed with laughing lines, had beamed as she had repeatedly said, 'I don't want to be any trouble. I want to help, not be a nuisance having to keep asking where things are.'

Raine sighed. Aunt Jo had come into the kitchen later and, while waiting for milk to boil for her nightcap, had taken off her pearl necklace. It was still lying on the draining board where she had left it. God knows, thought Raine, what the drawing room will look like. When she'd peeped in to say goodnight, seen that her aunt was comfortable and had all she needed, the small polished tables glittered with rings, necklaces, bracelets, and treasures, tipped from a roomy handbag. They would stay there, and no doubt be added to, until the room looked like an oriental bazaar. Fortunately Jo, as she preferred to be called, didn't mind in the least having to sleep on a sofa-bed. She kept insisting she didn't mind anything, she was easygoing. But it made Raine angry to think there was a good bedroom upstairs that on police orders could not be touched.

Now in the kitchen, Raine put the pearls on the table where Jo would see them, but not where they would be in

Jeffrey's way when he came to breakfast. It would be no use unburdening her irritation on him. He'd only say, as he had several times lately if she complained about anything, 'You're too damn fussy.' It wasn't like him to speak like that. He used to think everything she did was cute, even when by a whisker she caught the toast from burning. But yesterday's barely burnt offering had become an issue. They argued over trivialities.

Today Jeffrey passed no comment from behind his newspaper that the toast was perfect, the coffee steaming. She scowled into her cup. When he'd finished and was ready to leave for the office he kissed her lightly on top of her head.

'Well, bye for now, darling. I won't have to worry about you today. I'm so glad you've got Aunt Jo.'

She tilted her face to give him a peck. That's what it had come to, she thought, after he'd left. She tried not to feel bitter. Perhaps it was her fault, she'd been on edge, hard to live with. But it wasn't all her fault, damn it. It was his damn daughter's. *His* daughter. Kim had come between them even though she wasn't there, damn her. Damn, bloody well damn. 'DAMN! DAMN! DAMN!'

Her invectives, with uncharacteristic venom, burst from her with the loudness of an explosion from a too-taut balloon. Jo appeared in the doorway. She took one look, then was in the room holding Raine tightly. After a few silent moments she said: 'Cry. Cry, Lorraine. Go on, cry. Let it all out.'

Raine felt the warmth of Jo's motherly body against her own. It had been so long since she'd had a woman to talk to. Involuntarily her chest heaved. She drew breath until she could hold no more, and her shoulders fell forward and shook and released her anguish in sobs and convulsive gulps so loud it seemed she would break her heart. When they gradually subsided, Jo eased herself away and in silence made fresh coffee.

'Thank you,' Raine said on a sigh. 'Not ... not just the coffee.'

Jo smiled from the opposite side of the table. 'Where

131

shall we go? A nice long walk in the country? Or look round your pretty village?'

'I never go to the village ... not since...'

'Then let's go together. I'd love to see it.'

Raine considered the idea. She had avoided meeting people by staying home. Now she felt as if she were stuck at the foot of a cliff, but would be all right if only she could make the first step up. 'Okay. Thanks. When I've washed up and run over the carpets.'

'Heavens, darling! Whatever for? Everything's already beautiful. I'd say clinical. But then, so's the hospital.' Jo laughed. 'If God wanted us to keep our homes so immaculate we'd be born with little vacuum cleaners attached.'

Raine managed a forlorn smile. 'Okay,' she agreed, and sipped her coffee. She recalled her aunt had always loved walking. With her felt hat worn askew she would stride so fast that Raine as a child could hardly keep up. Raine wondered if at fifty-six her aunt was still as energetic. At least, Raine realised with a resurgence of affection, her aunt was the kind of person she could tell everything, who would listen, perhaps even understand. She put down her cup. On impulse she poured out her troubles. Her pent-up feelings, the guilt, the mental torture, her fears. She was more aware than before of the lines round Jo's smiling eyes and mouth, as if etched by living, and understanding. Probably even in part a legacy from India, China, and Japan which in her zeal for life she loved to visit and bring back gifts. Raine said:

'I'm scared to death by even the sight of that Inspector Robeson.'

Jo smoothed her greying hair. 'But my darling, you mustn't be, when you have no need. It's his job. He's only doing his duty.'

Robeson was indeed at that moment in the police Incident Room on duty. He commanded the attention of a number of detectives who pored over paperwork, answered phone calls, and occasionally joined in the general crossfire of questions and shared information. He called to Detective Constable Mike Searle: 'Mike, about Miss Barclay's car she sold.'

'Yes, sir. Swansea came up with his name and address.'

'I know that.' Robeson's disciplined impatience was obvious; he merely wanted Mike to recount the low-down he'd learnt as a result.

'Apparently he works on a ship. A 10,000-ton ferry. It does a regular run from Draymouth to the Canaries.'

'That mean someone's going to get a cruise to the sun, sir?' Sergeant Mills cut in.

'Not for the moment, Roger. It sailed five days ago. With about three hundred passengers, and a cargo of God knows what. Brings back tomatoes. We'll wait till it gets back in seven days time, and just see...'

'Pity, sir. I fancy a few days in Tenerife. Doing the old flamenco.'

'Hard luck then, Roger. Best we can do for you is London's East End.' He noted the corners of Roger's mouth turn down. 'See a Michael Teed. Father of a youth Jeffrey Croft killed in a car accident. You'll have all the relevant information.'

Superintendent Moore arrived to give his daily briefing. He addressed Robeson: 'Howard. Your trip yesterday to question John Watson. Do I take it we're on to nothing?'

'He's living with a new girlfriend, sir. Rather nice sort. We caught her on her own. She gave him a perfect alibi.'

'Credible?'

'Seemed so. Apparently he's a rep for a flour firm. He made several business calls in Draymouth on the thirty-first. His last call was about six o'clock at a mill just outside. He was home about seven thirty. After a meal he went to the pub about eight thirty.'

'On his own?'

'Apparently, sir. He was home again around half past ten. The girl couldn't be exact about times.'

'And you later saw the man himself?'

'Yes sir. We waited. Neither the girl nor he had known

we were coming. But questioned independently, all their answers tallied.'

'And your impressions?'

'Seemed genuine. Watson admitted to having made threats to Kim Croft. It was in the heat of the moment. Though he says he hasn't, and never will forgive her for dragging him to court on a false charge.' Robeson paused. 'He called her a she-devil. Said she probably deserved whatever's happened to her, if anything has.' Robeson looked at Inspector Starks. 'Quite a day, wasn't it, Mary?'

Inspector Starks looked up from thumbing her notebook. 'It certainly was.'

Robeson continued, 'Watson reckoned Kim Croft probably monkeyed around once too often. Perhaps chose the wrong guy. Watson said she'd have a man's flies undone in ten seconds flat. If she hadn't had his trousers off first.'

There was a general tittering among the men.

Robeson said, 'I asked him about his relationship with Monica Croft. He said he had been serious. Until the daughter tried to come it. He couldn't be responsible for a girl like that.'

'Seems fair enough,' Moore said. 'So you think he's clear, Howard?'

'Well sir ... Mary timed the journey. We took the main road going. Another route back. For time, there was nothing in it. About an hour.' He paused. 'Watson, according to both of them, went to the pub about eight thirty and was home about ten thirty. In two hours it would have been just possible for him to have come over to Drayford and get back home again.'

'Did you check his story in the pub?'

'Yes, sir. He was seen there. But earlyish. The landlord couldn't confirm how long he stayed.'

'Same old story. The pub. They can never bloody remember. What's your gut feeling?'

'I think the man's genuine, sir. Can never be hundred per cent. Seems settled with this girl. Nice type. I wouldn't think he'd do anything silly.'

134

'And you, Inspector?' Moore looked at Mary Starks.

'I agree with Inspector Robeson, sir. In fact, until Watson heard about Kim Croft's disappearance...' Mary referred to her notes, 'He said he had absolutely no idea she was in this part of the country.'

The Superintendent concluded his briefing, then left them to get on with the nitty gritty.

Robeson gave a loud sigh. He knew Inspector Stark's conclusion, and for the moment he agreed. Her reckoning had proved sound in the past. But as he glanced at the roomful of detectives he wondered when the bloody hell they, and he, were going to make a breakthrough? He kept much of his personal speculation of the case to himself. Every scrap of information, however small, he regarded as a possible vital piece to store in his ragbag mind. But he expected his subordinates to come clean with every snippet so that he might interweave them. He had to catch every tiny detail that would make everything else make sense. He sat up straight on his hard chair, and changed tack with an open question for all to hear:

'These witnesses who saw William Pym on the night of July the thirty-first, the night the girl went missing...'

'Ten or ten fifteen, sir.' Mike Searle was quick with the information.

'Bugger the time, Mike, we all know that. But was he wearing a jacket?' Robeson hated stalemate, he was impatient to get things moving. 'We've established he was not wearing a jacket when his body was found five days later. His mother made a right song and dance about that. But was he wearing one when seen going up the village?'

There was a rustling of papers and general assent that Pym was wearing a jacket that evening.

'Right.' Robeson stored the confirmation in his mind as if it were a squirrel's nut he might want later. He said: 'Now. What's new?'

Several men spoke at once. Robeson interrupted: 'Don't bloody well tell me about the psychics, the clairvoyants and water-diviners. I've had them all up to my bloody balls!' He noted their differing expressions and reassured: 'They're being dealt with. Their suggestions taken seriously. You know we're obliged to investigate every lead.' He noted PC Drew from the local police house had joined them. He said: 'Any fresh pub talk, Trevor?'

'No sir. The fingers still point at the chap they all called Bible Billy. They reckon subsequent events prove something.'

'Hm,' Robeson grunted.

Inspector Starks said, 'The entry in Pym's exercise book for July the thirty-first ... do you think ... it sounds almost to me...' She was aware several men looked up from their papers to listen. 'He might just have had some ... well ... very close encounter with her.'

'Spell it out, Inspector. Are you trying to say sexual intercourse?' Robeson said for all to hear.

She didn't appear to flinch at his hint of sarcasm, but produced a photocopy of the relevant page and read: 'It was in my mouth sweet as honey: and as soon as I had eaten it, my belly was bitter.'

Robeson stroked his chin. Lots of pairs of eyes were raised from their desks.

She said: 'After all, sir, he follows that on August the first with, "God be merciful to me, a sinner", St Luke, 13.' She paused. 'And then he adds from St Luke, 26, "For this thing was not done in a corner".' She almost always respected his rank, called him 'sir' in front of the others.

Robeson went on scratching his chin. Mary Starks had something. He'd always admired her intellect.

'Well, just suppose for a moment you're right, Inspector. Why should he get rid of the girl after he'd had his wicked way?'

'I'm not suggesting he did, sir.'

'Did what? Did away with her, or have his wicked way?' Robeson liked statements made diamond clear.

'I'm not saying he did anything to hurt her, sir.'

'Then Jesus Christ, what the hell are you trying to say? Pym hung himself, didn't he? Why?'

She remained calm. 'Perhaps it was like in that short story, sir. *Rain*, by Somerset Maugham. I expect you know it.'

Robeson's recollection was vague, he'd never been a great reader of fiction, though anything about birds... He said: 'Listen chaps, Inspector Starks is going to tell us a story.' His scepticism sounded round the room as clearly as his voice.

She wasn't put off. 'There was this prostitute, Sadie Thompson. And a missionary, Mr Davidson. They were stuck on a South Sea island. Samoa or somewhere.' She paused. 'But I'm sure you all know it.'

'Then refresh our memories,' Robeson said, not admitting he hadn't a clue.

'Well Davidson tried to convert her to Jesus. Make her mend her wicked ways. He made his wife and friends pray for her. He read from the Bible the bit about the meeting of Jesus Christ with the woman taken in adultery.' She stopped.

'Is that it?' Robeson asked, disappointed.

'No. Then he spent nights in her room, praying.'

'He could tell that to the marines,' chuckled Detective Sergeant Mills.

She grinned. 'Praying *with* her.'

'Strewth! Gets more porno,' Mills chuckled again.

Robeson glared.

'Sorry, sir. Thought she said he was *playing* with her.'

They all chuckled. Mills was a bit of a card, Robeson had to admit, if only to himself. He said, 'Go on, Inspector.'

'Well, he was a miserable sanctimonious old sod, this missionary. Far Holier than Thou. After nights of praying in her room he claimed he had transformed her soul. For the first time ever, his eyes shone with ecstasy.'

'Ho ho!' Mills exclaimed and stopped short.

Robeson snapped: 'Where's this leading us, Inspector?' He couldn't bear to waste time.

'Well sir, one night, in her room, praying to Lord Jesus to forgive her sins, to grant her His great mercy, bla bla bla ... well ... he himself apparently strayed.'

'Strayed?' Robeson barked.

'Well, succumbed to her evil way,' Inspector Starks clarified. 'Next morning he was found on the beach. Lying at the water's edge with his throat cut from ear to ear. His razor was still in his hand.'

'Huh,' Robeson grunted. 'But why do you think it took Pym *five days* before he endeavoured to atone for his sin? If sin he did.'

Inspector Starks shrugged. 'He admits to sin on his entry of August the first. He writes *God be merciful to me a sinner.* And on August the fourth, *The wages of sin is death.*'

Robeson grunted again and looked at his colleagues. 'Any ideas why Pym waited five days before doing away with himself, if indeed he did have anything at all to do with this girl?'

Mills said: 'Well, it must take courage, sir. It's said to be the coward's way out ... but really it's not, in my book.'

Inspector Starks said: 'D'you think perhaps, in the meantime, he told his mother? I mean, perhaps just told her he'd been out with a girl?'

Robeson couldn't hide his irritation. 'She would hardly have told her son to go and jump in the lake ... or rather, hang himself, would she?'

'Well ... we've both met her.'

Robeson recognised what she implied. 'Yes. Of course. I'm hardly likely to ever forget. William Pym didn't have girls. His mother forbade him. He was a loner.'

Sergeant Mills piped in: 'My gran always said it's the quiet mice that nibble the cheese.'

Robeson glanced his way. Trust Mills. But he had a point. Turning to Starks he said: 'You don't suppose his mother knew more than she let on? Her manner was extraordinary.'

Starks shook her fair head.

Robeson recapped on what had happened when he and Mary had called on the Pyms. 'When the old man broke down, he wanted a smoke. That wasn't allowed indoors. You went with him out into the back yard. Was there any sign the ground might have been disturbed?'

'No,' Starks said. 'I took a good look. As I reported, Pym sat on a box. I sat on an upturned galvanised bath.' She produced another notebook, and read from some random notes. 'Garden. A pocket handkerchief of sun-baked clay; a few lettuce gone to seed. The cracked ground looked hard as rock.' She paused. 'I remember thinking it would've taken some digging.'

'But a shallow grave possible?' Robeson queried. 'Clay soil takes no time to look hard again this weather.' He respected her judgement when she again shook her head, and he decided for the moment not to pursue the matter. It was a relief to know that when Inspector Starks was on a job, she needed no prompting on what to look out for. He mused on how it must be for a woman to have brains and beauty, too.

'Well now,' he addressed the room. 'Anything else worth chewing? Any more late informants?'

'A phone call, sir. Negative really. The girl wouldn't give her name. And probably what she had to say wasn't worth much.' It was Mike Searle reporting. 'On July the thirty-first, about eleven, eleven fifteen, or could have been half-past, she really couldn't remember the time for sure, she was with her fella around the side of The King's Arms. It's dark there, round the corner. Even the little light above the church lych gate was out. They heard someone shuffle by.'

'So what?' Robeson snapped as Searle's voice dropped. 'Which way did the person go, why was he or she shuffling?'

'End of story, sir. They didn't notice. Too busy canoodling. I tried to press her, sorry sir, unfortunate turn of phrase, I'll begin again.'

Robeson waited.

Searle said: 'She said she was with her back to the wall, her fella in front, and he's taller than her so she couldn't see anyway.'

'Thank you, Mike. Bloody helpful.' Robeson paused, then called: 'Any more gems of enlightenment?'

'Yes, sir.' It was the local constable. 'The baker told me about his table-hand.'

'What's that in plain English?'

'A dough puncher, sir. On Thursday, the first of August, when he was coming to work, he passed someone ... probably a man because he looked to be carrying something heavy.'

'Whereabouts, carrying what?' Robeson snapped, he was getting impatient.

'He couldn't see. It was dark. He was riding his pushbike without a light.'

'Why, and where, what time?'

'His battery was down. He nearly collided with someone walking in the middle of the road.'

'Did you ask where exactly, Trevor?'

'Yes, sir. On the right-hand side of the church as you go down the village and on towards the main road where he comes in from.'

'Where does this chap live, what was he doing on a bike? I thought everyone had cars these days.'

'He lives in a cottage out on the main road. He used to ride an old motor bike until the neighbours complained.'

'Complained?' Robeson raised an eyebrow.

'Well, wouldn't anyone, sir, woken by the noise of a kick-start, right under their bedroom window at three o'clock in the morning?'

'Bloody Hell, I'd say so. What sort of chap? Reliable?'

'Perfectly, sir. I often look in the bakehouse on my shift. Specially cold winter nights for a warm-up, and a mug of char.'

'Then get back to him, Trevor. Try and make him remember exactly what he saw at that unearthly hour.'

'Will do, sir. I'll try to catch him before he finishes work at midday and goes home to sleep.'

Robeson gave final instructions: 'Make him think hard, Trevor. And exactly how big the thing was that someone was carrying. And exactly where did he meet him? Find out, without making any suggestion, if it was anywhere near where the fields start ... and the hedges ... on the

140

left-hand side going down the village ... opposite some small cottages.'

Robeson kept his mounting suspicions under his mop of brown curly hair. A vandal wouldn't steal silently through the night to return a ladder.

14

The search for Kim Croft went on. The huge operations mounted to try to track down various cars seen in the area on the 31st July, had so far drawn a blank. But police horses still searched the heathlands around Drayford. And policemen, both uniformed and plain clothes, were familiar figures as they still trudged the lanes and byways. They looked around allotments and gardens, peered into sheds and, armed with questions and clutching clipboards, knocked on doors.

But newspapers had gone on to other things. And some villagers were now more concerned about when they were going to get their village hall back. It was difficult for local organisations to find an alternate venue for their meetings, and for the Whist Drive that had been arranged to benefit the Church Window Restoration Fund.

In the meantime, Aunt Jo had induced Raine to accompany her down to the village. They hiked from one end to the other and were intrigued by old cottages, cobbled squares, and iron pumps. They followed the brook as it meandered its weed-choked way in the gully beside the street, until it was no more than a ditch under the hedge beside the fields. From the open doorway of an old forge, they felt the heat from the fire as they watched the blacksmith supporting the hoof of a heavy horse between his knees, and drive home rectangular nails to secure a new iron shoe.

In the Post Office, Jo smiled at everyone in the queue for pensions and stamps, and wished them 'Good morning.' She was soon chatting to everyone in general as she selected picture postcards from a rack. She enthused: 'Isn't this village absolutely charming. It's my first visit here. I'm staying with my niece.' She inclined her head towards Raine. Raine responded to friendly smiles from people she had been afraid to look at. The same thing happened in the baker's shop. Jo proclaimed to customers, and to the assistant in a white coat and pancake hat behind the little glass counter: 'Mmm. Doesn't it smell gorgeous in here? This scrumptious hot yeasty smell of real bread!' Sniffing, she did a cheeky imitation of a Bisto Kid of her youth. 'It's my first visit here. I'm staying with my niece.' She indicated Raine. She bought a small crusty loaf shaped with four points like a King's crown that the assistant called a *coburg*. Then she decided she was absolutely gasping for a coffee.

She steered Raine into the Tudor Café next door. There a middle-aged couple were being served. Jo took the adjoining table and was soon remarking on the pleasant aroma of real coffee, the welcoming gleam thrown from the bright reflections of the horse brasses on the wall, the interesting beamed ceiling, and the cheerful tables with their red-and-white checked cloths. She introduced Raine and herself to the proprietress as well.

The following day, Jo wanted to explore Draymouth. Raine drove her own new car for the first time, and parked it near the docks. She didn't care for the mixture of indeterminate smells from the boats and warehouses, the grease and dust underfoot, and having to avoid falling over mooring ropes as they walked along the quay.

Jo was interested in everything: flags of origin, home bases, and what cargoes were being unloaded as derricks and grabbers swung overhead. She watched young dockers working, their muscular bodies bronzed and half naked. From time to time foreign seamen came down a gangway; they sauntered along the quay and, with her command of languages and her beaming, uninhibited capacity for making friends, Jo asked them where they were from, and where would they be going next?

She learnt what cargoes they brought. She passed the information on to Raine; sometimes cargoes included corn gluten pellets, soya bean meal, fish meal, sulphate of ammonia, bagged urea, whatever that was, and sunflower pellets. Jo wouldn't leave the boats before repeating what she had learnt about them, and reading out their exotic names: *Eugen Rothehenhoefer*, of German origin, arrived from Szczecin, Poland. The *Star Libra* from Rotterdam. The *Galtide* from Cyprus that was about to sail in ballast to Fowey. And the Honduras *Oriend* just arrived from Germany for a crew change.

Raine wondered what the seamen thought of Jo in her pink cotton dress, heavy walking shoes and, in high summer, her black felt hat perched askew on her greying head. They appeared to respond amiably enough to her questions, so probably realised she was just an inquisitive, but harmless, mad Englishwoman.

Raine was relieved when at last she was able to steer Jo away from the murky, smelly water; it floated with dull rainbows, cigarette packets, and bobbing flotsam. But only a little later, in the town, Jo cried: 'Look, Raine! Antiques!'

Raine's heart sank; Jo was attracted to a narrow side street, drab and lined with small, shabby-looking shops. But she automatically turned into it with her aunt. There was litter in the gutter. She glanced away and, with a sense of irony, read on the wall the name of the street: Paradise Row.

A uniformed policeman was doing a bit of old style 'back on the beat'. With measured, leisurely steps he trod the narrow pavement, looking as if he hadn't a care in the world. Here, one shop after another sold antiques. Bedroom furniture, porcelain washbasins decorated with flowers, jugs and chamber pots to match, and marble-topped washstands. There were buyers and sellers of old silver; collector's items, memorabilia. Shops that dealt exclusively in very old clothes, antique lace, shawls, and Victoriana. Junk shops with notices, *We buy and sell anything*. Shops with large notices scrawled in chalk across their windows: *Secondhand clothes. Goods taken, Sale or Return.*

'Lorraine, my darling, why haven't you told me about this absolutely gorgeous place?'

'I've never seen it before.' Raine wouldn't have mentioned it even if she had; to her, antiques were not just old, they usually looked filthy and smelt musty. She glanced resentfully at The Bargain Shop with its window crammed with junk, and was glad when at last she was able to drag Jo away from the area, get back to the car and make for home.

They were passing the village Post Office when Jo said: 'Stop, Raine. What's that big notice in the window? I didn't see it before.'

They both got out to read the handwritten poster. It advertised an event to raise money towards the church's new window. 'One should support these things, Lorraine darling. It's no good living in a village if one is not of the village.'

A few days later, when Drayford's fund-raising church fête was to take place, the weather turned cooler. Raine glanced at the clouds; they drifted like wisps of muslin across the sky in a soft breeze and kept hiding the sun. She tied a blue Alice band around her long brown hair, considered the possibility of a shower, and whether her sandals would be suitable for walking around stalls in a grass field.

She had never been to a church fête before. The smell of freshly cut grass mingled with that of people, and miscellaneous produce for sale. There were diesel fumes from a generator brought in on a lorry to drive a small merry-go-round.

She saw the wizened Reverend Potter, and a local television newsreader who had opened the proceedings. Amid friendly clamour, she bought a small jar of home-made chutney, and some local honey.

She couldn't tear Jo away from the craft stalls; small water colours by local artists, painted vases, and costume jewellery. There were stalls with handmade teddy bears, embroidered tablecloths, and canvas peg-bags made by members of the church. On the Women's Institute stall there were hand-knitted clothes; bonnets, bootees, and matinee coats. Raine passed them without a second glance; she did not want to be reminded of babies.

Nor did she share Jo's enthusiasm for trying to guess the weight of a pig; she wasn't desperate to win the prize of a bottle of home-made parsnip wine, and she didn't like to see the pink animal imprisoned in a pen. She was sure the grunts from the fat creature were protests directed at the ring of gawping people.

She left Jo and wandered to the other end of the field, towards the sound of excited shrieks and calls of children taking part in organised games. She joined the spectators who, in loud voice, were spurring on young competitors in sacks which they clutched to their waists; they bobbed up and down and forward and sometimes fell over in their efforts to reach the winning post. Then there followed the three-legged race, and the egg-and-spoon. Raine felt more relaxed than she had for a long time. She stayed until she knew it was time to look for Jo, who had earlier insisted that they really must have a cream tea before they left.

She turned to go. And then she saw him. Just a few feet away. He stared at her with hooded eyes; his black curly hair a mat above his red face, his grubby check shirt strained over the beer gut that bulged over his trousers. She glanced away, but just the sight of the horrid farmer had spoilt her day. He lurched her way, brushed past with a low, sinister mutter: 'You know where the girl is, don't you? You bugger.'

She went cold. So it was he who had made those phone calls, frightened her stiff. She could only suppose he'd done so because she had expressed her views on intensive farming. But everyone was entitled to say what they thought, it was a free country. It was absurd that he had taken so much exception, harboured ill feeling and tried to persecute her. But there had been no more calls since Bible Billy's death. She had presumed the caller, like everyone else, took that awful event as proof of guilt. Now it seemed the horrible man, on seeing her for the first time since their encounter in the farmyard, hadn't been able to resist his jibe. She supposed he hoped to get some satisfaction from her reaction; the look on her face, fear in her eyes, or the startled cry of fright she had denied him as an anonymous phone caller.

She had told only one person about the phone calls. Now if she identified him, Aunt Jo would want to report him to the police and have him summoned. Raine wanted no more involvement with the police. It would be only her word against his.

Upset, she saw no one properly through the crowd. She passed the stalls, only vaguely aware of sounds in the background; voices, catcalls, people laughing. Strident music almost drowned the childish shrieks, whoops, and yelps of delight of those who rode brightly-painted horses, or imagined they were driving sleek model cars on the merry-go-round. Behind it all sounded the monotonous chug of the generator.

'Raine!' Aunt Jo clutched her arm. 'Raine my darling, I've been looking for you.'

Raine hadn't seen her coming.

Jo lowered her voice: 'Lorraine darling, I don't think we should stop for tea.' She led Raine towards the five-barred gate where they'd come in. 'It's down this way, isn't it, the village hall, the Police Incident Room? We have been asked to contact them if we have the slightest information that might help.' She opened her big handbag and held it out for Raine to see inside.

Raine's scalp tightened, she felt suddenly sick, she couldn't believe what she was seeing. She walked alongside Jo, past the ice-cream van at the gate, and out of the field. She had only been in the police Incident Room once. That was with Jeff two weeks ago to see how the search was going. All those men at desks, those raised eyes, fathomless looks. She had felt she was on trial and had wanted never to set foot inside there again.

Jo said: 'I bought them for 50p!'

Raine knew there was no mistaking that the ear-rings Jo had in her bag – jade, the size of an old penny, with a Buddha in relief – were those she had given Kim. She stopped walking, her voice shook. 'Jo. Do we really have to? They'll tear me to bits. I can't remember telling the police she was wearing them, I didn't see her go out.' Raine felt ill at the prospect of more questions. 'Can't you just keep them? Say nothing. Must we drag it up?'

Jo touched her arm and gently steered her on. 'Lorraine my darling, we must. Leave it to me. You didn't know Kim had them. Sometimes she did help herself to your things, didn't she? Without your permission. And you certainly don't go to your own box of jewellery every day to see what's missing, now, do you?'

The Incident Room was as Raine remembered. Detectives in shirtsleeves leaned over desks, looked up, eyebrows cocked. They answered telephones, and bantered across the hall.

Jo asked in her beautifully-spoken voice, with no sign of nerves: 'Could I please speak to Detective Chief Inspector Robeson?'

Sergeant Mills said: 'Sorry, mam. He's not here. We expect him shortly. But what's the problem? We can deal with anything.'

'Oh, I'm sure you can. But I would rather like to see your Inspector; would you mind very much if we wait?'

'You can wait by all means, mam, if you don't mind. Take a seat.'

Jo explained: 'You see, my niece and I have been tramping all afternoon around the church fête. Thirsty work. And there's nowhere nice to sit down. So I don't really want to go away and have to come back.'

'That's quite all right, mam.'

'In fact, would you mind terribly if I eased off my shoes?'

Mills smiled. 'Not at all, mam. Go ahead. Feel free.' He looked round at his colleagues. 'In fact, would you like a cup of tea?' He welcomed any excuse for a brew.

'Oh, that would be wonderful. Are you making?' She paused. 'Have you got Earl Grey?'

Mills blinked. Tea was something brown and wet that came in a mug. 'Er ... probably Co-op ... or PG, mam.'

'I'm quite sure that will be absolutely delightful. It's very kind of you.'

Raine marvelled at the way Jo always brought out the smiles in people. It was the same when the Inspector arrived. Jo introduced herself so pleasantly and with such confidence that Robeson in turn seemed almost human, his restless dark eyes softened, and he said: 'Thank you very much for coming along.'

Jo carried on: 'Well, really, officer, when I saw these earrings marked 50p! I mean, how often would you find anything like them on sale in an English village?' She laughed, and the pleasant sound went round the hall and several men looked up unable to hide wide smiles.

She repeated, 'Fifty pence! They're antique! I paid the earth for them in China. I admit they probably saw me coming, people do,' she laughed. 'I said to the woman behind the stall, "Is that right, only 50p?" and she seemed quite curt; I didn't mean to offend her.'

'Could you describe her?' Robeson asked. 'So we can trace who donated them?'

'Oh yes, I took special notice. Though you'll think I'm very unkind, I don't mean to be – she was rather a plain woman. I'd say in her sixties. Tallish. An odd shape ... well, up here.' Jo patted her chest. 'And she had straight grey hair, and no chin.'

Robeson produced a small plastic bag, opened it and held it towards Jo to drop in the earrings.

Jo grinned. 'They're mine. Don't forget I paid 50p!'

'You shall have them back, Miss Barclay. For the moment, I'll have them.'

'They won't suit you,' she joked. 'By the way, I believe I heard someone address her as ... I think ... Mrs Pym.'

15

Robeson felt that Miss Jo Barclay had indeed been helpful. Such an intelligent little woman. She didn't ramble and digress as so many informants did. She had been concise, and stated her observations clearly. It had been a pleasure to listen to her perfect enunciation and to watch those humour-filled blue eyes. Even her old-fashioned cotton dress, heavy walking shoes, and that odd black felt hat, did nothing to detract from her congenial personality and obvious reliability. How different, he thought, from her niece, Miss Raine Barclay, whose every scrap of information in the past weeks had had to be dragged from her, and even then was dubious.

He decided to wait until the church fête was over before going to see Mrs Pym. He'd give her time to clear her stall, and do whatever else she had to do, and get back to her own home.

It was early evening before the field had been emptied by lorries and pick-ups of trestle tables, the tea-tent, the merry-go-round, the generator. The last of the helpers, mainly women, straggled off with their arms full, or trundled babies' prams piled with cardboard boxes.

Robeson made his way on foot to 43 High Street. After the blare of the fête, the village seemed dead. The Tudor Café, the Post Office, and the baker's were closed, though Drayford Family Stores obviously stayed open all hours. He paused to watch a starling trying to drink from the meagre water that trickled between the stones in the gully beside the road. He marvelled as always at the bird's purple and bronze-green iridescence, and thought, God knows when I'll get back for a decent session with

Draymouth Naturalists, to watch from the hide.

He crossed a tiny cement bridge to number 43 and, with the stiff flap of the corroded letterbox, he tapped on the drab brown door. It was opened by a tight-lipped Mrs Pym.

'Good evening, it's Chief Inspector Robeson, CID; I expect you remember me.' He observed her hostility. 'I would like to ask you one or two questions. Perhaps it would be better if I came inside.'

She pursed her lips and looked down her sharp nose. 'Wipe your feet.' She moved aside for him to come into the narrow hall while she shut the door behind him. 'What do you want to know?' She looked down at his shoes then pushed past him. 'Better come in front room, I suppose. If you've got clean feet.'

Robeson hoped his business wouldn't take long. He almost filled the room with its four walls of faded roses, and involuntarily blew out his thick lips to dispel the smell of mould, damp, and old furniture. The sooner he got back into the fresh air, the better. He said: 'Mrs Pym, I understand you have been helping at the church fête today.'

She faced him, arms folded over her large shapeless bust. 'I certainly have. I serve the Good Lord at all times. For redemption and for all His forgiveness and for His gracious mercy…'

'Yes yes, Mrs Pym,' Robeson interrupted. 'What I wanted to know … I believe you sold a pair of jade earrings to a lady.'

'So what?' she snapped.

Robeson didn't miss the flush that rushed to her flabby cheeks, the faint pink that passed over her receding chin and down her neck. 'I understand items for sale are donated. Can you tell me who gave you those earrings?'

She drew her thin lips back against her teeth and sucked.

Robeson followed her gaze around the room he remembered, with its biblical pictures, ferns and whatnots, and the old-fashioned hearth with its fire laid. Still no light came from the window hung with dreary lace curtains. He thought, if it wasn't for the maidenhair fern that filled the

151

deep sill and flourished a lively green, he'd say the entire place stank of death.

He waited, then repeated: 'Can you tell me who gave you those earrings? Can you remember?' She didn't look the sort of person who would forget anything. Unless she wanted to.

'Of course I remember. I gave them myself.'

Robeson concealed his reaction, this was better than he'd dared to hope; he'd half expected her to have feigned forgetfulness, or in some way pass the buck. 'Then may I ask, where did you get them?'

'I found them.'

'Where?'

'Is that any of your business? Does it matter?'

'Yes, Mrs Pym. It does. You say you found them. If they weren't yours, why didn't you take them to the Police Station?'

'Why? Should I have?' There was steel in her eyes.

'Of course. Because they weren't yours.' He waited. He could stare at the iron face as hard as she could stare at his. 'Exactly where did you find them?'

'They were in my son's jacket pocket.'

My God! he thought, is this true? What mother would try to implicate her son? 'Are you sure?' He noted her sneer was almost triumphant.

'You should know. If you don't, you lot don't do your job properly.' She pursed her lips and twitched her shoulders, looking haughtily pleased. 'You came here with that chit of a girl. Asking nosy parker questions. Just like you are now.' She sniffed. 'Pretended you wanted to see if my son had left a note. You said you'd look in his jacket. I'd told you it was down the church.'

Robeson remembered. At the time, he had to look for only a note; any personal possessions of William Pym's were of no concern. From memory Robeson recalled there had been a large key attached to a wooden tag, and what one might expect to find in any young man's jacket pocket, some oddments that jangled. 'How did your

152

son come to have them, did they belong to his young lady?'

'William had nothing to do with strumpets! I forbade it!'

'Then how? It's not usual for a young man to have earrings in his pocket. Unless of course he had bought them to give to some young lady.'

'William would have done no such thing! How dare you! He was a decent follower of our Lord Jesus Christ!'

'Then what would you have done if he had told you he had, in fact, been seeing a girl?'

'I'd have sent him away to bathe, to scrub himself. To cleanse his whole body in the river Jordan!'

Robeson ignored her scarlet-faced outburst verging on hysteria. 'Then can you please explain how your son came to be in the possession of earrings?'

'He must have picked them up. Of course. Picked them up. Probably in the churchyard. He was always tidying up. For the love of our dear Lord Jesus Christ.'

'Then if they didn't belong to him, why didn't he take them to the Police Station?'

'Perhaps he would have. But our Dear Lord called him. So I was selling them for the benefit of the church that William loved, wasn't I?'

'But they weren't yours to sell. Keeping by finding is stealing. Isn't there a commandment on that?'

She pursed her thin lips and drew in her weak chin till it merged with her neck. 'You can talk. You police. I know you. Keep things three months to see if they're claimed.' She twitched her sloping shoulders. 'If they're not, who gets them? Not the honest person who took them in, I'll be bound.' She sniffed, and sucked her teeth. 'You're all the same.'

'Your views don't excuse your keeping them. Is your husband, Mr Pym, about? I'd like a word.'

'He's out in the lavatory.'

'I can wait. I don't suppose he'll be there all day.'

'He will if I don't say he can come in. He wanted to smoke his filthy old pipe.'

'Then perhaps you could show me your back garden. I would like to see it, please.'

She backed to the door as if to bar his way. 'I don't see what right... Invading my privacy.'

'Mrs Pym, I've got an investigation to conduct.' He noticed she hesitated in face of his firm stand, then with bad grace opened the door. He followed her, conscious of the stale smell of past cooked meals that pervaded the dark passage, kitchen and tiny scullery.

Outside, he took in at a glance the small plot with its narrow cinder path to the clothes line and a tumbledown shed. It was surrounded by a six-foot high wooden fence, providing privacy of which he couldn't imagine anyone would wish to deprive her. He noted the upturned galvanised bath which Inspector Starks had said she had sat on. Next to the scullery window, from over a door that was about eight inches short at top and bottom, there escaped tobacco fumes from Mr Pym's malodorous pipe.

Robeson saw the lavatory door opened. He reintroduced himself to the small balding man who came out, obviously attracted by voices: 'Good evening, sir. Inspector Robeson, as you know. I came to ask your wife about something she sold on her stall at the church fête today. And I decided I'd like to have a look at your garden.'

Mr Pym removed his pipe. 'Mother does it. More energy than me.'

Robeson didn't miss the look of animosity his wife shot the stooping figure in crumpled trousers and brown woolly cardigan. He turned to Mrs Pym. 'Managed any turning lately?'

She pursed her lips and jerked her shoulders in irritation. 'Certainly not. We've had no rain for weeks. And what's there to plant out? Are you a gardener?'

Robeson wasn't. But his rule was to ask all the questions, not to answer them. He surveyed the starved-looking garden with his keen eyes, and guessed his boys wouldn't be very pleased if he sent them in to dig this lot up. He scrunched up the cinder path and peered in the shed.

Thick cobwebs were unbroken, the hard-packed earth floor undisturbed. Nothing seemed untoward among the pots of dead ferns, buckets, an old bike, a clothes-peg bag, and a plastic washing basket. He dredged up his mental diary. On Thursday, the first of August, young Pym had written in his red exercise book: *God be merciful to me a sinner*. And *For this thing was not done in a corner*. Robeson returned to Mrs Pym waiting arms akimbo beside her husband. 'Have either of you been able to recall what your son did on the Thursday before he died?'

'No,' Mrs Pym answered for both. 'I suppose you mean the Thursday before the Good Lord called him?'

'He was praying, Mother.'

'Shut up, Walter! The man doesn't need to know that. No interest to anyone what William did in his own house.'

'Oh, but it is, Mrs Pym. Can we talk inside?' He would have preferred to stay in the air, but felt they could be overheard. He watched Mr Pym tap out his pipe and leave it on the scullery window sill before going in.

In the front room, chill with sanctimony, Robeson looked down at the freckled head fringed with white hair and asked: 'Did you hear your son praying, Mr Pym, or did you assume he was because it was usual for him to do so?'

Pym's wife snapped: 'William wasn't well that day. He stayed in his room.'

Robeson kept his eyes on Mr Pym, waiting for him to answer.

'I heard him, sir. Loud. Louder than usual.'

'He wasn't well, I tell you!' Mrs Pym pushed herself between him and Robeson. 'But he was better Friday. And Saturday. He went out. He must've picked up the earrings on Saturday because I cleared out his pockets Friday.'

'Didn't you look in his pockets on Saturday?'

'No. He'd left his jacket in the porch. Down at St John's. I was always telling him about that. Make it grubby one of these days, I said. Against that old wall!'

'What about Sunday?' Robeson asked.

'He went to church, of course.'

155

Robeson surmised by her tone of aggressive pride that she would have stuck out her chin, if she had one. 'Didn't he need his jacket?'

She drew herself up. 'To church? On a Sunday? My William wasn't a heathen. On Sundays he always wore his two-piece suit!'

'I see. So his jacket would probably have been hanging in the church porch most of Saturday and remained there until you fetched it.'

'Exactly!' She sucked her teeth. 'In the meantime, on the Monday, you, nosy parker Inspector, had to go down there and rummage through his pockets, to see if William had left a note.'

'We were extremely sorry, Mrs Pym, to have to do that. We hate to intrude on grief. But unfortunately there are times ... when there's to be an inquest ... it has to be done.' He saw the defiant shrug of her shoulders. He said: 'What about the Sunday?'

'He went to church, how many more times do I have to tell you?'

'Sunday, he was very quiet, Mother.'

'Shut up, Walter.'

Robeson saw the old man pass the back of his hand over his stained moustache, and heard him sniff. 'Did you notice anything else, Mr Pym?' he asked as kindly as he could.

'I heard him praying out loud again. After church. In his room. Didn't I say to you, Mother?'

'You talk a lot of tommyrot!' To Robeson she said: 'You said you came about earrings. Are you satisfied now? If so, I'll show you out.'

'For the moment, yes. And thank you for your time. You have both been very helpful.' He inclined his head to show them courtesy, but his smile didn't reach his eyes.

His head buzzed with ideas and suppositions as he made his way back to his car parked outside the Incident Room. After all the wild rumours, had the girl after all run away and managed to lie low? When he had first questioned Miss Lorraine Barclay, she had been sure Kim had not

156

absconded. Then she had changed her story and remembered Kim had threatened to scarper if her father sent her to boarding school. He bit his lip. He was normally reasonably patient, you had to be to enjoy his particular hobby. But Lorraine Barclay had been a time-waster, there were occasions when he had seriously considered that she and the girl's father could both have been involved in Kim's disappearance.

There was still the possibility the girl had been abducted. There was no evidence that she was dead. If eventually she was found to have been murdered, would it turn out to have been a senseless killing, on impulse, for someone's perverted pleasure, or...? He ran his fingers back through his hair as he racked his brain. Who had a motive? He went over his interview with Mrs Pym and pondered on the possible outcome if she had found out that her son had indeed met Kim Croft. Surely Hell would have no fury like that monster mother defied.

He reached his car, unlocked it, got in and pulled away slowly without bothering to look in the Incident Room. Enough was enough for one day; he didn't want to add to the list of broken marriages in the Force, and he reckoned Janet had been long-suffering enough.

It was still light. As he drove his familiar twelve miles home, he was fully aware that Drayford and its surroundings were farming country. He had spent farm holidays as a boy, riding on tractors, and making hay. He knew, as August merged with September, the fields of barley, usually left standing until the grains are fully ripe and the ears bend down, would be ready to harvest. Now he would have to make sure that workers in charge of combine harvesters were again reminded to be on the lookout, to keep an ever-watchful eye in front of their cutting blades. And as they cleared their barns of straw, to continue vigilance for Kim Croft.

16

Robeson always welcomed a new day. In the case of Kim Croft, he hoped for some fresh development, the chance that his diligence, or that of his team, would result in a new lead. Perhaps to help them there might even transpire some happy coincidence, or they would unearth a nugget of information quite by accident.

It seemed no such luck was forthcoming. In the Incident Room he drummed his fingers on the table, and considered the heads in front of him. As he listened to reports and comments, his frustration mounted. He barked: 'I want some fresh bloody ideas!' He noted fed-up scowls. 'I know it's paperwork. Over and over. Cross-checking. It has to be done. Go back over the ground. Speak again to witnesses, bring them back in; those lads that were outside the pub that night; they saw Kim Croft follow William Pym out from the saloon bar. About nine twenty. Did they really see Kim Croft catch up with him? Did he push her away as if he didn't want her company? Or did he put his arm round her? Take her hand? Lads like that don't usually miss much.'

He paused to consider further. 'Did Pym and the girl turn in round the corner, to the church? Because according to the vicar, and Pym's mother, that was where William Pym would have been going. To lock up.' He paused again. 'And just how much noise were those lads kicking up on the forecourt of The King's Arms, say for the next hour?' He barked: 'You want to know *everything!*'

He surveyed the nodding heads and waited a moment for his words to sink in. Then his glance fell on Sergeant Mills. 'Now, Roger. Yesterday you interviewed a Michael Teed in Stepney?'

158

'That is correct, sir.'

'And you're convinced that nothing he said needs pursuing?'

'That is correct, sir. The London boys had been there, too. Their patch.'

'But you didn't go all the way up there for nothing?'

'Not entirely. I saw Teed. He said he'd like to have got his hands round Croft's neck if he'd had the chance. Or his daughter's. He wasn't fussy which one. To pay the bastard out for killing his son.' Mills paused and looked at his notes. 'But he knew nothing about Kim Croft's disappearance. Had the perfect alibi. On July the twenty-sixth he was remanded in custody for a week for GBH. I checked that.'

Robeson grunted. 'Well, anything new on the girl from the London end?'

'No sir. According to them, apparently no one who knew her in her home town, neighbours, schoolmates, or anyone, had seemed surprised she was missing.' Mills paused. 'There seemed a lack of concern or interest. At least, that's what I thought. No heartbreak. Suppose you can't blame them. It sounds she was always a right bugger.'

Robeson glared. He hated heartlessness at the best of times; he certainly didn't encourage it among his subordinates, and he was in no mood this morning for flippant opinions. He barked: 'Sergeant, if it were permissible to rid society of anyone thought to be a right bugger, a lot of us might not be here.'

Mills smirked.

Robeson wanted only hard facts, possible motives, anything that might offer a lead. He turned towards the door and snapped almost before the local PC had time to come in and close the door behind him: 'Morning, Trevor. Have *you* brought any new bloody ideas? How's gossip?'

'Nothing new, sir. Same forgone conclusion.' He paused, then as afterthought: 'Someone in The King's Arms did mention little Mrs Retter's funeral. As you know, that was Thursday, first of August. People say Bible Billy was conspicuous by his absence.'

Robeson was fed up with stale news. 'Pym wasn't well that day apparently. Didn't go out. So his mother says.'

'It's just a case of find the girl then, isn't it, sir? At least we know the culprit. If she's found harmed.'

Robeson's dark eyes flashed beneath bushy brows. He thumped the table with his heavy fist and fixed his glare of outraged authority on the surprised young constable. He blared: 'It's not usually difficult to see the bloody obvious, lad! And if you're ever hoping to get on in the Force, never be too ready to accept what looks bloody obvious.' He stood up and strode from the room. He didn't usually let his patience snap, but he'd scheduled his day, and it didn't include wasting blood pressure.

Outside, he paused to take a deep, calming breath; extreme irritation was no mood in which to be going to interview a certain Kevin Parr on the ferry due back from the Canaries. Robeson climbed into his car, pulled smoothly away and drove down the village. Reaching the main road, he crossed it to take the minor road to Draymouth.

He had done his spadework. The captain and a senior officer expected him on board, and he'd timed it well. The three hundred or so passengers had disembarked, and the quay was almost clear of cars when he drove on. Dockers were already unloading crates from the hold. Loaded lorries pulled away. Robeson made his way up the gangway, and extended his hand to the officer waiting. 'Good morning, sir. Chief Inspector Robeson, CID.'

'Good morning, Inspector. Captain Jim Lang.'

On board, men were carrying out maintenance. Stewards and other staff went about their various duties. Captain Lang apologised: 'Sorry it's a bit like Clapham Junction. We do a quick turn-round. Sail again this evening. But you can be assured of privacy below, if you don't mind going down?' He indicated to a lad to show him the way.

They descended two flights of polished wood, then iron stairs that to Robeson with his fifteen stone to manoeuvre, seemed near vertical. He followed a narrow passage below the waterline to Kevin Parr's cabin.

Even in the poor light afforded by a diesel generator to compensate for the lack of a porthole, Robeson could see that the man who waited, seated on his bunk, looked frightened. Robeson said: 'Mr Kevin Parr?'

The swarthy man stood up.

'I'm Chief Inspector Howard Robeson, CID. I expect you have been told I'm here to make some routine enquiries.'

The man nodded and, with a bandaged right hand, indicated a chair that must have been especially provided, filling the cramped space. Robeson found it much better than standing almost head to ceiling.

Parr sat down again. Robeson with the speed of flashlight absorbed every detail; the thirty-year-old man was not relaxed despite his casual appearance – jeans, a sleeveless navy singlet, with a thick gold necklace, and hooped earrings.

Robeson asked: 'How did you hurt your hand?'

'An accident.'

Robeson studied Parr's face; one side was bruised and scratched; weals continued down over his neck and one of his heavily tattooed arms. 'And your face and arms?'

'Sure. Same.'

A man of few words, thought Robeson. 'Where? What exactly?' he asked.

Parr sounded offhand. 'Las Palmas.'

Robeson judged the weals fairly fresh; perhaps a week, but they could have been older. 'When did it happen?'

'Forget. Perhaps a week...'

Robeson thought him terse and elusive, though surprisingly well-spoken. He asked: 'Was it a fight?'

'Oh no.' Parr paused, but as if he realised more was expected, he added offhand, 'I fell off the cradle.'

'Cradle?'

'Thing we hang over the side, to stand on. To paint the boat. Rusts like hell else.'

'And you got all those scratches, being fished out of the water?' Robeson asked, only half believing.

'I got jammed. Some boat came in alongside. I didn't know what happened. Till I was being clawed back.'

161

Robeson nodded. He knew all the signs of tension, but that explanation could so easily be checked it would have been hardly worth falsifying. He changed tack: 'Now, Mr Parr, what I really came about ... can you tell me everything you did in Drayford on the evening of Wednesday, thirty-first of July?'

Muscles tightened round Parr's mouth. 'I went to fetch a car.' Defensive, he added: 'I'd paid a deposit on it. The Saturday before. When I saw the advert.'

'That was at a house at the end of a long lane, wasn't it?'

'That's right.'

'What time exactly ... when you fetched it?'

'I can't remember.'

That answer sounded too quick to Robeson, as if Parr had no intention to remember. Robeson said: 'Then think.'

Parr raised his voice: 'You're trying to pin me, aren't you? I knew it! When they said you were coming. I knew it.' He leaned towards Robeson, their knees nearly touched. 'I never hurt him! I swear to God I didn't. He ran right out, I braked but he tripped. He picked himself up at once and ran on, or I'd have got out to see if he was all right.'

'What are you talking about?'

'I swear I would've. I was stopped. I'd stalled. I couldn't get going. Not at first. It was the car. Not being used to it. But I'm sure I didn't hurt him.'

'Who's he?' Robeson couldn't follow.

'You know very well. Don't come that. Or why else you here?' Parr rested his right elbow on his left hand, holding his right hand erect as if it were hurting. 'I swear he ran out. I swerved and braked. Lucky nothing was coming.'

'Mr Parr, what are you talking about? Will you tell me where you say this person ran into the road in front of you?'

'No. I can't. I don't know.'

Robeson wondered if this was a convenient mental block. Parr seemed put out. But he was a tough-looking man, he must have experienced rough situations and this incident, if true, sounded comparatively minor. Or was it a yarn to head off any reference to Kim Croft? Robeson waited:

Parr said: 'I don't know that part very well.'

'What part?'

'Drayford. Where I bought the car.'

That sounded reasonable. Robeson said: 'Mr Parr, you saw this man sufficiently to swerve out of his way. In fact you actually stopped, you say. What did he look like? Tall, fat, or short? What was he wearing? Shirtsleeves, jacket, or did he have bare arms? And where did this sudden apparition spring from? Your left, or your right; in which direction were you driving?' Robeson felt he'd given Parr plenty to think about. He waited:

Parr said: 'He came out of the dark.'

'Do you mean from the turning up to the church?'

Parr hesitated. 'I don't know where the church is.'

Fair enough, thought Robeson, he'd got the picture. 'Well, what can you remember about his appearance?'

Parr thought a moment. 'I think he might have been tallish. And young.'

'His clothes?' Robeson prompted. 'A dark suit, a light suit, shirtsleeves?'

'I ... I'd say lightish ... yes ... I think a light suit.'

'Or perhaps darker trousers, but a light jacket?'

'Well ... yes ... possibly.'

'And you saw no one else? Absolutely no one? Take your time, Mr Parr. Think hard.'

'There was a crowd outside the pub. Under the fairy lights. People laughing and singing. I nearly went back. To ask someone to give me a push.'

'And didn't you?' Robeson asked.

'No. I opened the door and stuck my foot out on the road. I kept my left hand on the steering wheel and pushed the car with the other.'

Robeson noted the man's voice had trailed to a murmur. He asked: 'What happened?'

Parr said nothing.

'Well, what?' Robeson repeated.

163

'It started,' Parr said.

Robeson scented more. 'Well, then what? Did you see anyone else?'

'No.'

'You're quite sure?'

Parr's gypsy face registered concentration. 'I didn't see anyone ... but I remember now ... I'd forgotten ... well, some times ... somewhere ... I thought I heard a shriek.'

'What sort of shriek, where?'

'I don't know. I only thought I did. There was a crowd outside the pub. I thought to myself let's get on.'

'Why? Does a shriek frighten you?' To Robeson the seaman's language was astonishingly mild, he hadn't sworn once.

'I didn't want to stop.'

'But you said you were stopped.'

'I mean I didn't want ... to perhaps get involved in some drunk's brawl. It wasn't my business.' He paused and put his tattooed left hand to his lips. 'But ... come to think of it ... that may have been the first time.'

'First time?' Robeson snapped.

'I'd stalled before. I suppose I eased up too sudden, coming on the pub, there were people nearly in the road.'

'You don't sound much of a driver, Mr Parr.'

'I didn't know the area. Or the car.'

Robeson let it go. Fair enough. Though one car was much like another to him. He said: 'Mr Parr, you haven't told me what sort of shriek you think you heard. Whose do you think it was?'

'Oh, a girl's. Screaming she was.'

'But you said nothing before about screaming. You only said you thought you heard a shriek,' Robeson wanted things black and white.

'Well ... it's coming back. A shriek. I thought I heard it. But then ... no more ... and then some screaming from somewhere ... I couldn't be sure ... so much noise around ... chaps near the pub, larking.'

164

'What's the difference, Mr Parr, between a shriek and a scream?' Robeson wasn't sure he could define it himself.

'Well ... the shriek was sudden like. Sort of shrill and piercing. It cut through the other sounds. Like the people laughing and singing.'

It sounded a good definition to Robeson, but he wanted Parr to expand on the original question. 'And what's your idea of a scream, Mr Parr?'

Parr frowned, looked stumped. 'Not much difference I suppose. But a scream's not so short and sharp. It sort of goes on and on.'

Good, thought Robeson. Especially for a man who, from the accounts he'd had of him, had been fostered all his life and now, of no fixed abode, shared his sleeping hours between his boat and the YMCA.

'Well, Mr Parr. I want you to think very carefully. Did you hear that girl screaming *before* you nearly knocked down a person who ran in front of your car, that is, the first time you stalled? Or did you hear the screaming when you stalled for the second time, *after* a person ran out in front of you, fell over, picked himself up and went on up the road past The King's Arms?'

'I didn't hurt him, I know I didn't.'

'That's not what I asked you. Did you hear screaming the first time you stopped ... which was apparently at a point just *before* you reached The King's Arms? Or the second time you stalled, which sounds to have been just past The King's Arms?'

'I can't remember.'

'Then think. It's very important.'

'I can't remember. The near shave shook me up. I could've killed that fella. But I didn't. So I put the whole incident out of my mind. Then they said you were coming. They didn't say what for.'

Robeson was anxious to press on. 'Do you think you could recognise the exact spot, or spots, near enough, where you were stopped when you thought you heard screams?'

Parr shrugged. 'Possibly. But I don't know.'

'I'll speak to the captain. Then I'll run you in the car back over the ground. It might help you to remember anything else.' Robeson paused. He felt it time he got onto the subject of Kim Croft, in case the man was shielding himself by inventing this incident. He asked: 'Are you sure you saw no one as you drove on down the village? I'll refresh your memory. There are cottages on the right, and some fields on the left, before you reach the main road, to come on to Draymouth.'

'I don't remember seeing anyone. I believe it was dark that end. No street lights.'

'You are quite right, Mr Parr. Then perhaps in your headlights you would have noticed anyone walking, all the better?'

'I expect so.'

'You didn't see at any time, from The King's Arms downwards, a young girl? Tallish. Thin. In a black leather miniskirt?' Robeson fixed his eyes on Parr for the slightest reflex. He saw none.

Parr said: 'No. If I had, I'm quite sure I'd have remembered that.'

Robeson stood up and ducked, his head nearly touched the ceiling. 'Right. I'll see the captain. You might as well lead the way out of this labyrinth.'

In the purser's office, alone with Captain Lang, Robeson made his request to take Parr to Drayford.

'We sail at six thirty,' Lang said.

'I'll have him back in good time, captain. I certainly can't hold him without evidence.' Robeson gave the impression he was ready to leave and join Parr who waited outside. But with a contrived casualness he remarked: 'Nasty weals and bruises he has.'

'Yes. Very nasty. He's been excused duties. Can't do much with a broken wrist. Hardly worth it, was it, for a cat?'

'A cat?' Robeson wondered if he had heard right.

'He dived from the boat-deck to rescue a ship's cat.' Lang gave a short laugh. 'Not even ours. Some dreadful wild

166

thing off some foreign tramp steamer that had no business even to come alongside.'

'Parr didn't say.'

'He's not the sort, apparently. He might look rough. I understand he has an excellent character.' Lang paused. 'I suppose it's like what they say ... about judging a book by its cover.'

Robeson caught the captain's shrewd eyes. 'Like hell! By his looks I'd expect a Harold Robbins. Not a Lionel Blue.'

'Been any help?'

Robeson grinned, and moved his head from side to side. A lock of thick curly hair fell over his forehead. 'He's got a poor memory. Perhaps when it suits him. I'm going to try to jog it.'

Robeson was true to his word. After taking Kevin Parr up and down Drayford village road, again and again, first in the car, and then walking, trying to get him to recollect the spot where he'd heard screams, Robeson drove him back to Draymouth docks, and saw him safely aboard.

Before leaving the boat, Captain Lang asked: 'Did you manage to jog Parr's memory?'

Robeson was cautious. He was going to satisfy no one's curiosity. His brain buzzed, and he had no intention of airing his pot-pourri of observations and ideas to anyone until he had sorted them out. He said: 'He's been quite helpful.' Robeson's mind was elsewhere. He wanted to do this alone. If he brought it off, Janet would be proud; it might make up for the long hours she'd spent without him, the spoilt meals, and their fractured, if non-existent social life. And he could do some bird-watching again with a happy heart. He said: 'But he still couldn't quite remember this, or couldn't quite remember that.'

'You suggesting he didn't want to?'

'No. I'd say he really tried to remember.' Robeson was thinking that Kevin Parr, like clutter kept in a cupboard in case it came in useful, had been on his brain long enough. Now disposed of, Robeson felt he could function

167

the better. He repeated: 'No, I think he really tried to remember.'

Lang said: 'I suppose you can never really be sure.'

Robeson agreed. But he felt smug. It had been a good day's work.

17

There was something about Drayford that really got to Robeson. The quiet, the sense of peace that was entirely missing from where he lived. Admittedly it was convenient to live fairly near his office at Divisional Headquarters. But here nothing had been commercialised. Even the comparatively small town of Draymouth, barely five miles away, with its long sandy beaches, had chain stores, supermarkets, and busy docks near the mouth of the estuary.

He supposed, as he took his customary morning walk to get some air before going into Drayford's village hall, turned Incident Room, there was always a price to pay for staying as you always were. Here children played in the street, or sat in their doorways. There were no play schools. No public park or gardens; even the fields belonged to farmers. And when school began, he understood that even toddlers were whipped off in a special bus to Draymouth for their education. He reflected that this place must then be as dead and bereft as Hamelin after the Pied Piper had done his worst.

Robeson was always reflecting; never off duty. Appearing to stroll aimlessly, his policeman's mind worked unceasingly. He noticed that some women apparently went straight from their kitchens to the shops, still wearing their flowered aprons. A milkman delivered by pony and trap, trustfully plonking down bottles and leaving them beside the road. In the morning light, The King's Arms looked unpretentious in spite of its beer-barrel tubs of begonias on the forecourt. From the open half of the saloon's sash window came the smell of stale beer and tobacco.

Robeson's walk took him to the churchyard. He would

never cease to marvel at its perfection. Here and there a grave was being tended, fresh flowers being arranged, the spent ones carried conscientiously to the bin. He reminded himself, as he saw the thick form of Fred Palmer just ahead, to be careful where he trod. 'Good morning, Mr Palmer. Working as hard as ever?'

Palmer straightened up from doing something to a grass-cutter. 'Oh aye.' He fixed Robeson with his red-rimmed eyes. 'You was 'ere t'other day.'

'That's right. You remember. You told me all about the church windows the vandals broke. And I admired the way you keep the grass.'

'Oh aye. Well, everything's same.' He sounded put out at having been disturbed again. 'I told 'e why I took broken glass 'ome fer the dustcart.'

'Yes. You did, thank you, Mr Palmer.' Robeson paused. Then using his most solicitous tone he said: 'In fact, do you think you've been quite fairly interviewed, and treated?'

Palmer nodded 'Oh aye.' His reply sounded grudging but definite.

'Well, if you are quite sure you have been fairly and courteously treated...' Robeson reached into an inner pocket of his jacket, 'would you mind signing this form?'

Palmer looked bemused. He hesitated, then held out his red, roughened hand.

Robeson said: 'Read it. Read it first. Just read what's on it.'

Palmer read the simple form that asked if he had been interviewed fairly, and appeared satisfied. 'Well, where...?'

Robeson produced a pen. He indicated an inscribed kerbstone right beside them, the grave itself having been cemented over. 'You could use here to lean on.'

Palmer steadied the form with his left hand, and signed his name.

Robeson thanked him and, after a few more moments of small talk he continued his walk back to the Incident Room.

* * *

170

It was just before eleven o'clock that a phone rang. Sergeant Roger Mills picked it up, listened, then without replacing the receiver, looked across the Incident Room to where Robeson was engaged with several colleagues in a little conference. By the sound of their guffaws and banter it was on more personal lines than police matters. 'Sir,' Mills called. 'It's PC Walsh calling from Draymouth. He's apprehended a lad carrying a Sony cassette.'

Robeson turned to him: 'So? Must be hundreds of Sony cassettes. Believe they call them Walkmans or something.' He had been interrupted from enjoying a particularly good yarn, and he didn't much want to go haring off somewhere on a wild goose chase. 'Any reason Walsh suspects it could be *the* Sony cassette?'

Mills asked Walsh, then reported his reply. 'The boy said he'd only just bought it. But he hadn't got a receipt.'

'Well, what's the problem?' Robeson snapped. 'The PC's got a bloody tongue in his head, hasn't he? Has he held on to the lad, asked him where he got it?' Robeson didn't bother to come over and take the receiver. 'That's easy enough to check. Dixon's, Curry's, Woolworth's. All packed with Sony cassettes. Their computerised cash registers spew out receipts like confetti.' He paused. 'And like those bits of paper, receipts are just as easily dropped. The boy's probably lost it.'

Mills paid attention to his caller for a moment longer, then replaced the receiver. 'It's not a new one, sir. Walsh is taking it to Draymouth police station. For possible identification in case it belonged to the Croft girl.'

Robeson left his party to join Mills. 'What's in the file on Croft's cassette?'

'Not much, sir. A Sony radio cassette.' Mills was already rifling through papers. 'Black. About eighteen inches wide. Clumsy. Quite big. And hard. Sounds verbatim from one of your interviews with Lorraine Barclay. You said at the time she really got up your nose.'

'Never mind her. That description fits thousands of bloody Sony cassettes. Did I say there was a name on it,

171

or any known scratch marks? I'm sure I didn't, but just check.'

'No sir. Nothing like that. Oh, hold on, sir.' Mills turned the page. 'There's a bit more to Lorraine Barclay's statement.' He read aloud: 'She used to take it everywhere. In here sometimes ... but sometimes she carried it with a strap from her shoulder.' He looked at Robeson. 'What did she mean by *in here sometimes*?'

Robeson paused to reflect. 'I remember. *In here* referred to a yellow canvas holdall. But ... about the strap ... do all radio cassettes have straps?'

'I don't know. Walsh said the lad was carrying it. I pictured he meant by a handle, but I could have got it wrong.'

'And where exactly did he apprehend this lad? I presume Walsh has got all details, name, address, and pedigree?'

'PC Walsh was on his beat, sir. In Draymouth. Before I put the phone down he said the boy had bought the cassette quite close to where he was apprehended. In a street called Paradise Row. From a second-hand bargain shop.'

'The second-hand bargain shop? Paradise Row?' Robeson pricked up his ears like a lost dog at the sound of its master. His revived interest was apparent to several of the officers who'd been listening. 'That's typical! It's amazing what you can get in that crumby shop. Perhaps that Sony *can* be identified, Roger. Get on the blower. See if Lorraine Barclay's at home.'

Robeson welcomed the excuse for a run around, even if there was little hope; he'd been getting grouchy here because things seemed stalemate. He crossed back to his side of the room to collect a book. He heard Mills get through. 'Tell her I'm on my way. I'd like to take her to Draymouth police station,' Robeson said as he left.

He knew the bargain shop well, as did most of his colleagues. Little of its stock was acquired through orthodox channels. The owner, Slimbo Ferris, had appeared before the magistrates more than once.

Robeson felt it wisest to take Miss Barclay to the cassette rather than the other way round. If it really was the Sony

172

that had belonged to Kim Croft, it would have been mauled already enough on its circuitous route to Slimbo's tatty shop. Perhaps it was too much to hope it might reveal identifiable fingerprints that were on file; but one had to be careful to preserve the possibility, however remote.

He had interviewed Lorraine Barclay many times. Now he had a legitimate opportunity for yet another encounter with the exceptionally good-looker who at first he had labelled suspect number one. In spite of his being fed up with her appalling way of giving information in small, grudging instalments, he wouldn't be a man if he didn't secretly admire her physical attributes; the slim figure, the proud tilt of her head, and the shoulder-length brown hair that was held back with ribbon from her serene face.

He took Inspector Starks with him to provide female company for Miss Barclay on their joyride to and from the police station in Draymouth. But he needn't have been so circumspect, he found Miss Barclay had the company of her Aunt Jo.

Expecting him, they were on the lawn of the large house at the top of Moor Lane. Enjoying the view that was out of this world, thought Robeson as he noted the garden chairs, padded and cretonne-covered; the swing sofa with scalloped canopy, and on the teak table a tray set with china for coffee and biscuits. He envied gracious living; some people had all the luck.

He said: 'Good morning. No, please don't get up,' he added, smiling and nodding to each in turn. 'As you already know, I'm Inspector Robeson.' He indicated Mary: 'This is my colleague, Inspector Starks.'

'You'll sit down, won't you, and have a coffee?' Aunt Jo said, already pouring from an exquisite jug with a long spout.

Smiling, they thanked her. Looking at Raine, Robeson said: 'I'm sorry to have to trouble you, Miss Barclay. But this shouldn't take very long. Can you tell me, is there any way you might be able to identify Kim's Sony? For instance,

173

can you remember if there were any special scratch marks on it ... or anything like that?'

'No. I don't think so. I never really took much notice. It was just black. Like any other.'

Robeson probed: 'Had it a strap? You said so in your statement. I haven't yet checked up, but perhaps you can tell me, do they all have straps?'

'I don't know.' She spoke slowly, as if it were something she had never considered. After a moment's reflection she said: 'But anyway ... hers wasn't a proper strap. I mean, it was a strap. She hung the Sony over her shoulder with it. But it was really a long belt. A narrow black leather belt she'd bought for the purpose.'

'Well, that should make identification easier, providing the strap's not been detached.'

They finished their coffee. Fifteen minutes later, at Draymouth police station, Lorraine identified the Sony, without doubt, as Kim's. The leather belt had been coiled, crossed with two thick rubber bands to prevent it from coming undone, and tied with string onto the handle of the Sony as an extra.

Robeson was satisfied that now, forensic would do its best. He returned the two Miss Barclays to their elegant home, and thanked them for their help. He would like to have skived for the rest of the day, driven to the banks of the estuary and enjoyed the company of waders; perhaps a brilliantly coloured kingfisher in the sandpits along the bank and, as the tide receded, long, orange-billed oyster-catchers with pink legs wading along the edge of the lapping water. But his mind was already working on his next assignment.

Robeson knew exactly where he would find Slimbo Ferris. If that squat man was not engaged in trying to find something someone, from among the jumbled and diverse stock that filled his poky shop in Paradise Row, his Pickwick-like stature would be filling the doorway. It was debatable to those who knew Slimbo, whether he was con-

174

stantly on the lookout for customers, or for a blue uniform with shiny buttons and a policeman's helmet, that might be coming his way.

Today was no different. Robeson, forced to park his car some distance away due to yellow-line restrictions in Draymouth's Soho, walked up Paradise Row to the second-hand bargain shop. He manoeuvred his way past displays of china basins and chamber pots that trespassed on the narrow pavement. The owners were always being warned about that, but it still went on. Nearing the bargain shop, he recognised the yellow waistcoat with its loud check, the black bow tie, and the deerstalker cap, the trademark of the proprietor who filled the doorway.

'How d'you do, Slimbo,' Robeson greeted him, noticing by the shadow of surprise that crossed Slimbo's face that he hadn't been quite ready for someone he knew was an officer of the law in plain clothes.

Slimbo nevertheless sounded his usual affable self. 'Good morning, sir. Or should I say afternoon? I was just off to have my lunch.'

'Perhaps you could spare me a few moments first, Slimbo? I'd like a word. D'you close for lunch? We could go inside and shut the door.' Robeson knew Slimbo never closed, he might miss a customer.

'Of course. Right away. It's Inspector Robeson, isn't it?'

'Right first time, Slimbo.'

There wasn't much room inside. Ferris pulled down a black roller-blind over the glazed upper half of the shop door, and with his foot tried to shift some clutter on the floor so that he could shut the door. He said: 'How can I help you, officer? I presume this isn't a social call.'

'Right again, Slimbo.' Robeson had a sneaking, if grudging admiration for a man never at loss; who had a certain charm and presence, and spoke with a public school accent. Robeson noted the way Slimbo twisted between his thumb and forefinger, his thin, stiffly pomaded moustache that curled up at each end to resemble an inverted eyebrow.

175

Robeson said: 'I believe you sold a Sony radio cassette player to a lad this morning?'

'I did, officer.'

'It was second-hand, of course. Who did you buy it from?'

Slimbo moved his head slowly from side to side, indicating he didn't know, or couldn't remember.

Robeson thought the man odd, still in his deerstalker; he never removed it. 'Come on, Slimbo. Of course you remember. And you damn well know appeals have been put out to anyone finding a used Sony radio cassette player, by any means, to inform the police?' He wondered as he watched the shaking head, how long Slimbo was going to keep up his act of amnesia. 'You must've heard the appeals, Slimbo. On the radio. And the description. And I presume you watch TV. And read the papers?'

Ferris twizzled his gold-tinted moustache.

Robeson pressed: 'With you it's a case of none so deaf and blind as those who don't want to see or hear, isn't it, Slimbo?'

'Oh, officer, really. Come off it. You're not being fair.'

'I am being fair, and you know it. A schoolgirl is missing. She was carrying a Sony radio cassette. All the papers carried full descriptions. They were full of nothing else just two or three weeks ago.' He noticed Slimbo's clean-shaven face take on a bemused half smile, as if he were working on his answer.

'Two or three weeks ago?'

'She went missing July the thirty-first. You must know that damn well.' Robeson was getting impatient.

'But this player was only brought in yesterday,' Slimbo said. 'I didn't connect. I get so much these days. Look! You can see I'm overstocked.' He paused, causing Robeson to look round the cluttered shop with him. 'The market's flooded. Every gadget under the sun's being produced small and computerised. Pocket computers to beat the bookies; backgammon computers small enough to slip in the pocket, with everything needed to play on the move. And so it goes on. People buy these miracles of technol-

176

ogy, don't know how to work the dratted things, and they end up brought in here.'

Robeson conceded the point. 'Well, Slimbo, I'm sure you can remember as far back as yesterday. Who brought in the Sony?'

Ferris curled the end of his moustache around his finger. 'No. I can't for the moment remember. Not to be certain.'

'Well, let's have what you do remember, for starters.' Robeson was going to get some sense from the man if it took him all day. 'Think, Slimbo. I want your full co-operation.'

'Of course, officer. You know me.'

Yes, too damn well I do, thought Robeson. But he kept that to himself. Ferris was being singularly polite, no doubt his way of trying to make up for earlier lapses, to get himself into the Force's better books. Robeson asked: 'What did the person look like who brought it in? Young or old? How much did you pay them for it?'

'Oh, I didn't pay anything.'

'What? Nothing?' Robeson couldn't believe his ears.

'I thought I told you, officer. I'm overstocked. At the moment. I'm only taking stuff sale or return. But I've refunded the lad's ten quid, I couldn't do fairer than that now, could I?'

'No, Slimbo. That's okay. We can forget him. But I still want to know who brought the Sony in? You took it sale or return?'

'That's what I said.'

'Then you'll have the name and address of the person who left it; that should help even more, if you're not going to give me a description.'

'I'm not sure I can even help you there, either,' Ferris looked towards a corner at the back of the shop.

Robeson observed papers piled high, under which was possibly a small but tall desk like one used in a Dickens' novel. 'I can wait while you look through that lot.'

Ferris didn't move. 'I'm not sure I gave a receipt. Some people leave things on trust.'

'Well, start looking,' Robeson said sharply.

The rotund man squeezed his way to the papers. 'I know I didn't ask for an address. Just the name. After all, they're bound to be back for their goods, or the money.'

'When's that likely to be?' Robeson asked.

'I only give them a month. If things aren't sold, and people don't come back to claim their property by then, I don't reckon to be responsible. It goes in my junk room for a while. And then...' He shrugged. 'It's anybody's if I throw it out.'

Robeson pondered the difference between Slimbo's junk room and shop. 'Do you get much stuff left on your hands, unclaimed?'

'Quite a bit. Surprisingly. People forget. Or go away.' Ferris searched through papers, letting half of them fall on the already littered floor.

'What happens to the money if you sell something and its owner doesn't come to collect?'

Ferris puffed as he bent to retrieve something he'd dropped. 'Well. It's here waiting. They get their money if they come.'

'And if they don't?'

Ferris grinned. 'Well. That's business.'

'D'you reckon you get much stuff dumped on you? I don't mean stolen goods that we usually ask you to look out for. Things that for other reasons someone might want to be shot of? For instance, this Sony. D'you reckon whoever brought it in and left it with you, sale or return, is going to come back?'

'I don't see why not.'

'Will you let us know immediately?'

Ferris stopped rifling among his clutter. His manner was that of a recalcitrant schoolboy wanting to make up to teacher. 'You know very well, officer, I'll do everything I can to co-operate. After all, it's no skin off my nose. I gave the boy back his money. You've got the player.'

Fair enough, thought Robeson. 'How was it brought in? Carrier bag? Brown paper?'

'Thick newspaper. Day before yesterday's local *Herald*. I remember that because of the big picture of our Carnival Queen on the front.'

'And yet you can't remember what the person looked like that brought it in?'

'I scribbled the name down. It's here somewhere.'

Robeson wondered how anyone so obviously well-educated could live this life in this dump. But despite his odd choice of clothes, and permanent deerstalker, the long-sleeved shirt beneath his yellow waistcoat looked spotless, and his black bow tie was crisp. Above the curve of his moustache, his plump pink cheeks shone as if freshly scrubbed.

Robeson waited.

Ferris said: 'Can I get in touch when I find it? It's just the name. No address. I was so sure she'd call back.'

'She?' Robeson hadn't given thought that it might have been brought in by a female. 'A girl? A woman?'

'Oh yes. A woman.'

'It was only yesterday you say. And yet you can't remember what she looked like.'

'No. I really can't. Not to describe her. Or what she was wearing. I don't take much notice. Not of the sort in and out of here.'

Robeson kept his eyes fixed on him, a silent command to go on thinking.

Ferris said: 'She couldn't have been much to write home about. Or I could tell you.' He paused. 'If it's any help at all, all I can remember is, she had grey hair.'

18

Things were beginning to cut a definite pattern in Robeson's mind. He had dealt with suspects, clues, the occasional coincidences, rumours, the whys, and why nots? He had questioned Lorraine Barclay up to three times a day, put the screws on plenty of shady characters whose alibis had been the slightest bit doubtful. In addition along the way he had drawn on the skills of the whole police circus – top bodies, experts, and forensic. Now with most of his questions answered, checked, and cross-checked, his conclusion was that Kim Croft had indeed been murdered. He was positive he knew just where, and by whom. But in spite of his certainty, he had now to convince his immediate boss, Superintendent John Moore. It was a task that he envisaged could be a rough ride, taking into account the subsequent steps it would entail.

He ate a hearty breakfast as usual, enjoying Janet's cooking and company. He needed that, he told himself, to set himself up for the verbal battles that might lie ahead.

Driving towards Divisional Headquarters, his mind revolved with facts and arguments he was going to put forward. His case lacked one point only. Motive. He regretted that. Motive was the word he always drilled into his colleagues. He'd say: 'Look for motive. Find the motive and you're halfway to finding your man.' Motive was always the first thing to look for, and in this case he could think of none. But he couldn't wait any longer to find that one omission when, by his reasoning, the rest of the jigsaw was all there.

He drove steadily. Now and again when a clear road allowed, he glanced at the passing scene. Summer was getting tired, grass verges were brown with dust, the trees looked thirsty. But his mind never strayed for long from the case he was on; it had become an obsession. He was reminded that some crimes were committed without motive. Others for reasons that remained obscure. And as for William Pym ... he had been young and healthy. Exceedingly good-looking from all accounts. Yet forbidden by his mother to associate with girls. Would his sexual frustration have been motive enough for murder? Had Kim Croft laughed at the handsome boy's innocence? Perhaps even belittled his inexperience? Women had been murdered for less. Robeson moved his head slowly from side to side; he didn't believe it. He never had. It didn't fit.

Divisional Headquarters loomed ahead; a hideous building, Robeson thought. He preferred red brick, not square edifices of whitish grey that looked washed out. He found a space to park, and made his way into the building that to him was a concrete honeycomb where uniformed and plain-clothes officers buzzed in and out of their respective adjacent cells. He knew he could have put his conclusions on this case to Moore in the Incident Room at Drayford; the Chief went to and from his office to Drayford once and sometimes twice every day. But Robeson wanted Moore's undivided attention. He wondered whether to go straight to see Moore in his important office, further along the corridor from his own less imposing sanctum on the third floor, or to get Moore first on the blower.

Robeson had long been free to make his own decisions. And he had put quite a few people away in his time. But there were limits. The action which he was about to propose was beyond his jurisdiction. And Superintendent John Moore was after all running this show. Robeson felt it was common courtesy before he went higher, to consult Moore and get him to agree with his own way of thinking.

Anticipating a possible verbal battle with John Moore, he decided he would do better to put his theory face to face. Less chance of having the phone slammed down halfway through an argument if Moore was unsympathetic to fresh concepts, or if other calls took precedence.

Robeson collected his files on the Croft case, and paused several moments to reflect. Then filled with purpose and determination, he squared his large shoulders and strode down the corridor, prepared to put his head into the lion's den.

To call Superintendent John Moore a lion was apt, in that he had teeth and could roar. Though physically, with his thick short neck, round head, and small eyes, he more resembled a bear. And like that endearing animal, he was good-natured only to a point. When it came to arguments he could tear anyone apart and, in Robeson's experience, seemed to enjoy doing so. Robeson sometimes supposed Moore's broken marriage had soured him; that living alone, scratching his own meals when he wasn't able to use the canteen, wasn't conducive to good temper. Moore was a difficult man to convince; he'd accept hard facts but not suppositions. Black was black. White was white. He rarely considered smudges in between.

They had been colleagues ever since Robeson had entered the Criminal Investigation Department some eight years earlier. Robeson liked him well enough, and they had a good working relationship, even allowing that Moore could at times dig his heels in and be an awkward sod. But after all, there was always the margin of rank between them, requiring Robeson to treat him with at least some little deference.

Nevertheless, moments later, confronting Moore seated at his large desk, Robeson lost no time in apologising for any intrusion. After the briefest salutations, he put down his files, found himself a chair, and commenced to disclose the result of his weeks of detection in the Croft case.

Robeson wasn't encouraged by the changing expressions on Moore's podgy face, the way he scribbled an occasional note that was obviously going to be used in some later point of argument. Regardless, Robeson pressed on with what in his considered opinion would have to be the natural follow-up to his findings.

'You must be out of your bloody mind, Howard!' Moore's tone implied he didn't want to hear more. He reached for something on his desk as if the interview was over before it had been given a fair hearing.

Robeson opened his mouth to protest but Moore interrupted;

'An exhumation? For Christ's sake, Howard! What the bloody hell for?'

'Because of the evidence I've stated. I believe the girl was murdered in Drayford churchyard. On the thirty-first of July. Around ten o'clock. Perhaps a little later. And that same night there was an open grave.'

'And what does that prove? You can't be serious.'

'Never more. My latest witness heard a shriek. Then screaming coming from that direction. About ten o'clock.'

Moore's small eyes almost disappeared between narrowed, fleshy lids. '*Around ten?*'

'Well, he didn't actually look at his watch. And the church clock doesn't strike. It disturbed summer visitors.'

'Howard! For what you're asking, you'll have to be more specific than that! And where *exactly* was this late witness when he heard screams?'

'Either just past The King's Arms ... there's a turning there up to the church. Or he could have heard them just *before* he reached The King's Arms.'

'Jesus Christ, man! What d'you mean? *Might* have been here, *might* have been there? What sort of bloody evidence is that?'

'It is possible to be unsure. I mean, from which direction a sound comes from. Many a time I've looked up at the sound of a plane, and seen nothing at first because it's been in a completely different place in the sky.'

'Quite possible, Howard. Planes don't stay still while you're doing your boy-scout spotting.'

Robeson wasn't amused. He was prepared for sarcasm but was not going to rest his case, and he wanted Moore to know it. He said: 'Where I lived as a boy there was a village roughly three quarters of a mile away on each side. I often heard church bells that I thought came from one village when in fact they were from the other.'

'Wind direction, Howard. Wind direction. And have you never considered echo? You know your trouble. Better get your ears seen to.'

Robeson pursed his thick lips and looked hard at him like a kid playing at *I'll stare you out*.

Moore snapped: 'All right. We'll accept that it is possible sometimes to be confused by which direction a sound is coming from.' He paused. The smile he gave went no further than the cynical twist of his mouth. 'In which case, the screams that were thought, from two positions, to have come from the churchyard, may not have come from that direction at all.'

'I've very good reason to believe that they did.'

'But none of the other reasons you've given for your preposterous proposal have convinced me.'

Robeson spoke with exaggerated deliberation. 'The girl was seen with William Pym just before dark. About nine twenty. They were seen going towards the church. Still together. She had put her arm in his.' He paused. He would convince Moore if it took all day. 'It was Pym's nightly habit to see everything in the churchyard was all right. Call it his voluntary, religious duty. He'd make sure there were no vandals around. He would lock the church door. And shut the yard gate.' Robeson paused, allowing time for every fact to sink in.

'And so?' Moore prompted.

'Pym was seen running from the direction of the church, about ten. On his own. Around the same time, but either just before or just after that, screams were heard.' Robeson thought he'd made things absolutely clear.

Moore snapped: 'Either just before. Or just after. About ten. What sort of evidence is that?'

Robeson sighed loudly. 'I've had to accept a number of different timings during this case! Around ten, ten past, quarter past, what the bloody hell! People don't go around looking at their watches every time they see someone.

184

They're not usually thinking as they go around their normal lives that a crime might be taking place and they should take notes!' Robeson's frustration mounted; these particular details were anyway irrelevant to support what he was telling Moore he wished to do, and for which he would like his support.

Moore fixed Robeson with his small eyes. 'If this person is so sure he heard screams, why didn't he report them at the time? Or at least within the next few days? Jesus Christ! There was enough bloody publicity for him to have been made aware those screams might have had some connection with the missing girl. The papers were full of her. And then what about all those appeals for information that went out on TV and radio? He couldn't have missed all of them.'

'Seems he did.' Robeson felt he had at least one small trump. 'He works on one of the ferries to Spain. Maintenance, painter, or whatever. He was sailing next morning. He knew nothing of this till I met him when the boat docked in Draymouth. While he was at sea, I'd tracked him down as having been in Drayford on the evening of July the thirty-first.'

Moore rubbed his big hands together as if he were washing them. 'I don't think we should dig up some poor soul on the strength of a boy seen coming from the churchyard. And some decidedly hazy yarn about screams, Howard. I suggest we wait a bit longer.'

Robeson had expected resistance. 'How long do you propose? We've already had the assistance of hundreds of borrowed policemen. Off the record, we've dealt with a couple of thousand statements, three thousand or so questionnaires, not to mention the thousands of enquiry forms.' He took a deep breath and continued to expound: 'As well you must know, police diving teams have searched hundreds of ponds, wells, and ditches. And for what? Bugger all it seems. And you say *wait*.'

Moore rested his clasped hands on the table and went on slowly washing them. He sounded unmoved: 'Soon it'll be easier to hunt, Howard. Who knows what might be revealed when foliage dies down and leaves are shed?'

'Bloody hell,' Robeson swore. 'At this rate I could be retired from the Force, first. And the person who did for Kim Croft could have gone from the face of the earth.'

'You mean scarpered or snuffed it?'

'The latter more likely.'

Moore stopped washing his hands and leaned across the table, showing more interest. 'But apparently he has already left this mortal coil, hasn't he?'

'Well, what if he has? Does that mean that the girl can be left where I'm sure she is? At this moment, this is a missing person's investigation, not a murder enquiry.'

Moore raised his clasped hands as if in prayer and bent his head, speaking into them. 'So you want the grave of a Mrs Retter exhumed? You said earlier that she weighed only four stone. And Kim Croft, an anorexic, weighed five stone. Are you saying both bodies are in the coffin?'

'No. I doubt that.'

'Then what in God's name are you saying? Why bother to have researched their weights?'

'I did play with that idea. But subsequent intelligence changed my mind. I had a re-think.'

'Well, in the first instance, had you suspected the coffin carrying Mrs Retter's body might have been unexpectedly heavy?' Moore asked.

'I put that question to the undertakers. They didn't think so.' Robeson had left nothing to chance, no pertinent question un-asked.

'But in your notes, Howard, you say a bier was used. Why was that? For such a short distance. Hardly a hundred yards from the church door.'

'The undertakers were a man short. William Pym frequently stood in. They'd sort of relied. But he wasn't there.'

Moore uttered what sounded a cross between a grunt and him clearing his throat. 'Well ... you might think Pym would have had good reason to see the girl safely buried. But perhaps at that he turned chicken.'

Robeson was not going to contradict what he could hear

Moore was thinking. 'Well sir,' he said, paying full respect as usual to Moore's seniority, 'Are you convinced now? What are you going to do?'

Moore hedged. 'It doesn't rest with me, Howard. Only Force Headquarters can approve an exhumation.'

'Of course. I know regulations. But I thought it proper to approach you first before I went ahead.' Robeson knew when to say what he thought was the right thing.

Moore considered a moment. 'Your reasons aren't very strong to put to Headquarters.'

'I don't agree. At this point we have only to ascertain where that girl's body is. And in that, I know I'm right. You can argue against it until the cows come home.' Robeson rammed home his point.

Moore seemed to consider slowly. 'Well ... perhaps ... on that score. Nothing has ever been found to suggest she absconded.'

Detecting Moore's weakening, Robeson pressed on: 'And it's impossible she was abducted by some monster in a car, even at that time of night, when she was seen in Pym's company going to the churchyard. Normal traffic doesn't drive through the lych gate.'

Moore nodded over his hands and made mmm'ing noises. He said: 'And since William Pym's suicide ... apparently everyone it seems knows he murdered her.'

'Everyone *thinks* they know,' Robeson corrected.

Moore showed surprise: 'And you know different?'

'I didn't say so. But one thing at a time. Let's *find* the girl. See that I'm right about her whereabouts, first.'

'You'd bloody well better be, Howard, if I back you on this. It's more than my blood's worth, or yours, if you're wrong. But you're absolutely convinced?'

'That is correct. I'm sure I know exactly where. And probably how, though that's less important. Dead is dead by whatever means.' Robeson paused. 'But I don't know *why.*'

'You mean you don't know of any motive?'

'I haven't yet found one.'

187

'*Now* you tell me!' Moore drew in a doubting breath. 'I was thinking I would put your theory forward. But … no motive … for something you can't possibly be one hundred per cent sure of in the first place? Isn't there a chance your whole bloody pack of cards could fall down?'

'A motive for murder is not the issue. We have got to find the girl. And I'm bloody sure I know where she is.'

'So you keep saying.'

'All my assertions are supported by facts. They should be enough for an exhumation order. How much more do you need to be convinced?'

Moore narrowed his eyes. 'I am convinced, Howard.'

'You don't sound it.'

Moore shrugged his bear shoulders, and doodled on a note pad. 'You will still have to convince Headquarters. And of course the coroner before he'll issue an exhumation order.'

'I'm conversant with the rules, sir.' Robeson emphasised the *sir*. 'Though thanks for the reminder. Taking delicate matters to Headquarters isn't something I do every day. Nor am I on back-slapping terms with the coroner. But I'll work on it.' Robeson guessed he sounded petulant.

Moore said: 'And this is just a missing person investigation, Howard?'

'That is correct. At the moment.' Robeson tapped his nose and gave Moore a wink; he could read anything he liked into that, and probably would. Robeson was not, after all his graft of the past weeks, going to be satisfied with doing half a job. But for the moment, an exhumation order was all he needed.

Moore grunted again. 'You make it sound all right, Howard,' he admitted grudgingly.

Robeson pressed on. 'How about it then? When I put it to Headquarters, are you going to back me up?'

'Hold on, Howard. You're still going too fast. Just think. There, you'll be up against a lot of clever people. What if, after all your arguments, the girl had simply been grabbed? Yes. Around ten o'clock if you insist. Some bloke, Pym if you like, intent on rape, and the girl had broken free and done a bunk?'

'I don't believe that. She'd have been found. Every Force in the country's been alerted. Kept its eyes skinned as vigilantly as a school nit-nurse with a comb.'

Moore hung on like a cat to a fish-head. 'Suppose you are proved wrong? What glory that? For me? For your chances of promotion?'

Robeson dismissed his long-held dreams of advancement, of seeing Janet's pride when he became a superintendent. He had to have the courage of his convictions. Perhaps now or never.

Moore cut into his thoughts: 'Well, do you want to go ahead? And bugger the chances?'

It sounded like an ultimatum. Robeson said: 'I thought I'd made my wishes clear for the past two hours. There is no alternative. It's a case of press on and be damned!'

Moore gripped his chin between his thumb and forefinger. 'Okay, Howard.' He issued one of his rare smiles. 'I'll back you. In fact I'll get on to Headquarters. You can go to see the coroner. Tell him we want an order.'

19

The fairy lights outside The King's Arms went out. The last street light soon followed. Drayford was asleep. At least, Inspector Robeson hoped so.

He had left doing what he felt was his moral obligation to do, as late as possible. Not that it was compulsory for him to tell Mr Anthony Retter that his mother's grave was to be exhumed; authority far beyond Robeson's had given the go ahead, and that was that. No objection from Retter would make any difference, but Robeson was sensitive to the implication; he'd lost loved ones himself, and how would he feel if the action was taken without so much as an apology from anyone, a little sensitivity shown?

In Retter's small living room with its brocade-covered table, old-fashioned black hearth, and china dogs on the high mantelpiece, Robeson had broken the news.

'Aw.' Ginger had said. 'My sss ... sister lined the grave sss ... so nice ... with ff ... flowers and that. And lots of pieces of green sss ... stuff all round. Like a carpet it was.'

But after Robeson's sensitively worded explanation that included the minimum of reasons, Ginger had accepted the facts with no fuss. He had then even ventured to open up and ask: 'Mm ... my ladder, officer, dd ... did it help ff ... for fingerprints?'

Without answering, Robeson apologised again for his visit, and relied on Ginger's discretion to say nothing to anyone. Not that it was likely to matter, Robeson thought, by morning all the proceedings should be over. As he left and stepped into the dark, Ginger had in turn apologised:

'Tis time Council give us some street lamps down this end.'

190

*   *   *

It was well past mid-night. Robeson imagined Fred Palmer having nightmares if he knew what was going on in his precious churchyard; the digging, and tramping of heavy shoes, perhaps the unintentional spoiling of grass verges cut and shaped with precision. But it was only a passing thought; Robeson was on to other things.

There was no moon. Across the burial ground a pathway, screened by two parallel strips of canvas, led into a larger canvas enclosure hollowed protectively around a single grave. Emergency lighting from lamps held by speedily erected beams and gantries flooded the area. Outside, gravestones that caught some of the artificial light from the centre of activity, stood like ghosts watching over their dead. At a distance around the perimeter of the holy ground, and in front of the lych gate, uniformed policemen, visible only as dark shapes with the occasional glint of a button or helmet, stood guard. There was always the chance that a few night owls in the community, either walking their dogs or up to watch the midnight movie on TV, might be attracted to the glow. Any who came to satisfy their curiosity would be politely steered away.

There was a distinct nip in the air, in contrast to the warm day. A fresh breeze caused a draught in the trees and through any gap it could find in the surrounding hedge. Having foreseen a possible long night, Robeson wore a polo-neck pullover beneath a tweed jacket that was thicker than his usual navy serge. He thanked God conditions were dry, and had been for some while; that was going to make things better for everyone, apart from the condition of the body which he was convinced would be brought out. But knowing the nature of the work ahead, he had guessed rubber boots would serve better than his shoes to keep out the area's renowned clay soil. Not that he himself would be involved in the actual slog of digging, he again thanked God.

He went through the entrance of the canvas walkway and followed the canvas-lined path to the brightly-lit central

191

enclosure. It was almost circular and roughly twenty feet in diameter. There was little standing room; a large mound of soil was being added to by two men wielding spades in a hole about seven feet by three. He watched them labouring, cutting into the soil with almost rhythmic splices, deepening the excavation. He mused how the more ghoulish-minded in the village, who had conducted their own trials by pub talk, might react to such a scene, if called upon to witness the dreadful deed for which they had found Bible Billy guilty.

Soon, Robeson was not particularly surprised to see Superintendent John Moore appear. He looked more like a bear than ever, dressed in a bulky brown anorak. With him, come to survey what looked like an arena for over-enthusiastic archaeologists, was the vicar of Drayford church. It occurred to Robeson that the Reverend Potter, frail and stooping, with his clerical collar inches out from his thin neck, and gaunt cheeks a deadly pallor, looked himself to be an early candidate for the big sleep. Why couldn't they have left the pathetic old sod in his bed, what good was his presence here beyond a gesture that he had accepted the police's authority.

Robeson edged back towards them to utter the usual polite greetings, and save them the trouble in case they had thought of coming to him.

Moore grinned, and glanced towards the cavity where the two workmen had almost disappeared from sight. 'Nearly satisfied now, Howard?'

'Shouldn't be long now, sir. I've been to see Mr Croft. Gave him no details. Except we had a possible lead to finding his daughter. I forewarned him he may be needed to make an identification. Poor b... What a torture for any father. It's bound to be a bloody gruesome sight, however much cleaning up they do first in the mortuary.' Robeson hadn't meant to swear in front of His Reverence or in the sanctity of the place, but he had a teenage daughter himself and he felt so strongly it had slipped out.

Moore appeared not to have noticed. 'And after that,

Howard, you think you've a murder to tidy up, just for the record?'

'Well sir, she was hardly likely to have put herself down there, and covered herself up like some babe in the wood.' Robeson knew exactly what Moore was thinking. The same as everyone else, that the case was already cut and dried.

'And you don't think it will be necessary after the coffin's been brought up for it to be taken to the mortuary?'

'That is my belief, sir. There's hardly the remotest chance a second body will be found in it. It's my hunch that underneath the coffin will be the remains of a mat of artificial grass.'

Moore until now had been intent on watching the churning spades, the growing mound of red earth. He had turned occasionally, a little, to listen. Now he narrowed his small eyes and he turned fully to face Robeson. 'And? Underneath?' With a degree of indignation he added, 'I trust to the powers that be, Howard, you haven't gone as far as this, on a hunch.'

Robeson ignored what sounded almost a threat. 'I'm staking my reputation on my belief that underneath that mat of artificial grass...' He didn't think it necessary to finish his sentence, and anyway the thought sickened him. He went on: 'A body-sheet's here ready, sir. The pathologist is standing by at the mortuary. When he's done what he has to, and others in attendance have done what they can, which is rather different, our lads will take Mr Croft along. It's a bl...' he stopped short, glanced at Potter and moderated his language. 'It's an awful thought.'

'And what do you expect from the pathologist?' Moore asked.

Robeson stroked his chin. 'God knows. But he's the expert. She hasn't had the protection of a coffin and shroud. She will have been crushed. On the plus side she hasn't been down there long. What ... four weeks? And there's so little moisture in the soil, decay shouldn't be too far advanced.'

'And cause of death, Howard, you reckon? Prior to being crushed?'

Robeson shrugged. It wasn't the time to be speculating, and Moore knew it.

The next two hours went to plan. The coffin of Mrs Anne Retter was carefully removed from the earth and set aside. The remains of Kim Croft's mutilated body were recovered from beneath what had been a sheet of artificial grass, and taken to the mortuary in Draymouth.

Robeson's correct assertion allowed for the swift re-interment of the coffin, and for the surrounding ground to be restored to its former neatness as far as was possible. Beams, gantries and lamps, canvas sheeting, and the rest of the paraphernalia brought for the exhumation, were all cleared away before morning.

In spite of having had no sleep, Robeson went early to the Incident Room. As he arrived, rubbing his eyes, files were being gathered together, Ordnance Survey maps that had been divided into sections for the searches were being removed. The atmosphere among the officers was like school breaking up at end of term. No serious work was being done. They regarded it as all over bar the shouting, with congratulations all round, and to Robeson in particular. He was greeted by Sergeant Mills.

'Sir. Just had a call from Slimbo Ferris.'

'You can forget it, Roger.' Robeson was too tired to listen because nothing Slimbo might have said would make the slightest difference now. 'Fingerprint bureau found that Sony as clean as a bloody whistle. Been washed and polished. Suppose Slimbo thought he'd get a better price. So you can tell me anything else, later. All I want to know now is how's the teapot?'

'Coming up, sir,' Mills made for the improvised kitchen.

Robeson produced the remains of the snack Janet had packed for him over twelve hours ago, in case he needed a bite in the night. He had been too engrossed with events to think about food. Now in lieu of breakfast he tucked into the cold beef sandwiches she knew were his favourite, and washed them down with the strong brew Mills produced.

It was still barely nine o'clock. Robeson knew his subordinates were well able to get on with the clearing up without him. It remained to him alone to clinch the task that he and they as a team had worked at this past few weeks. His natural pride at a job well concluded was mixed with a twinge of gloom for the subsequent wretchedness it was bound to bring to others.

Drayford was still only half awake. In the fresh light of a new day he was satisfied that in the churchyard, everything would probably appear normal to the casual observer. But far from perfect to the discerning eyes of Fred Palmer.

Robeson didn't regard himself as sentimental. But he allowed himself time to reflect on Drayford churchyard. Yew trees shaped with precision, grass as velvet smooth as a bowling green, and clean paths. Rose-covered trellis screened the water containers. A bin for dead flowers and the wrappings of fresh blooms brought to replace them, had been painted green to blend with the surroundings. Borders planted with pink geraniums, and beds of fragrant roses where the burial ground had not yet reached, were kept more beautiful than in any garden he had ever known.

He bit his lip and, as he shook his head slowly from side to side, a lock of hair fell over his forehead. He rubbed his eyes. They felt hot and dry from lack of sleep. It was regrettable, he reflected, that grass grew so quickly, and that weeds, like naughty children with no one to check them, would soon take over. Even he thought it a shame that within such a short time, Drayford church had lost its verger, then Bible Billy.

And now Fred Palmer.

Robeson found Palmer in a far corner behind the church. He was pruning some roses, and looked up as if by instinct he knew someone was coming.

Robeson noted the open-neck check shirt, the white ring

of skin around his suntanned neck, and the truculence on his red face.

'Good morning, Mr Palmer. I expect you know why I'm here.'

'No. You was 'ere t'other day. I wrote me name on yer bit o' paper. You tell me why.'

Robeson fixed him with eyes that didn't blink. Palmer knew exactly why. He'd accused Pym of murdering Kim Croft. A good act that hadn't worked. Now his own guilt was blatant.

'Mr Palmer. Will you come along with me to the Station? I have evidence to believe that you murdered Kim Croft on July the thirty-first. You have no need to say anything, but I should warn you that anything you do say may be taken down and later used in evidence.'

Palmer took a deep breath. 'Be you bloody arresting me?'

'Well. If you don't come, yes.'

Palmer threw down his secateurs, lumbered a few steps, and sat down on a broad granite memorial. Once there he took a black handkerchief from the pocket of his baggy trousers and wiped his face and the back of his neck.

Robeson waited.

Palmer's lips curled. 'The dirty buggers. Both of 'em.'

'Mr Palmer,' Robeson interrupted, 'you don't have to say anything.'

'Why bloody not? I only come 'ere that night to try to catch they lads. They thinks it's funny to empty me bin and scat rubbish all over the place.'

'You can keep all this for the court, Mr Palmer, it doesn't help now.'

'It were just dark. But you gets sort o' used to it. An' I'd 'ave knowed 'e anywhere. Like a dog with a bitch 'e was.'

Robeson didn't want to hear.

But Palmer went on 'I 'adn't a bucket o'water, or I'd 'ave chucked it over 'em. So I give 'e a clout with me spade an' 'e yelped and flyed off.'

'You do realise, Mr Palmer...' Robeson began, knowing this was all stuff for the courts.

But there was no stopping the man with his gravelly country burr, wanting to unburden himself, eager to purge himself of what must have weighed heavily.

'I 'spected 'er to follow. P'raps 'er would 'ave. Would've been all right, then.' He paused, as if what happened next was not planned. 'Her started to run ... then 'er come back to me. Right banged up against me. Don't know what 'er idea was, but I pushed 'er away pretty smart I did.' He paused, and wiped his face and neck again. Then he rubbed his black handkerchief around his red-rimmed eyes as though crying. He said: 'And then 'er laughed. An 'orrible squeaky laugh. An' 'er said I wouldn't be man enough. An' 'er laughed again.' Palmer had been looking into the distance, his eyes, red-rimmed and rheumy, seeing beyond the peaceful, holy surrounds. Now he glanced at Robeson. 'I'd heard a laugh like that before. Years ago. An' 'fore I knew it, me 'ands were around 'er neck. I didn't mean to kill 'er, but 'er mocked me. With that laugh. So I squeezed till it was just a gurgle an' she flopped, an' I knew what I might 'ave done.'

Robeson noted Palmer's renewed truculence.

His thin lips curled, he looked a ball of anger as he raised his voice: 'But then I weren't sorry! *They was copulatin' in my churchyard*, weren't they? *Sacrilege in my churchyard! It's mine!* And I don't let no one defile *my yard!*' He paused. 'I pulled me 'kerchief off me neck and put it round hers to finish the job. I yanked it tighter an' tighter.' He paused again, almost breathless, as if he had just re-enacted the strangulation. 'Then I didn't know what to do.'

Robeson realised Palmer wanted to talk and was damn well going to, and to Hell with cautions. The facts gushed from him like water from a burst pipe. It crossed Robeson's mind that one day Palmer might even be saying he had had a confession bullied out of him; that he had had pressure put upon him. Yes, Robeson had heard that one before.

'Come with me now, Mr Palmer.'

Palmer didn't move from the granite stone. 'I'll bide me time.'

Robeson sensed the quietness. Only in the distance could he hear faint sounds of the village, the occasional car, and somewhere a cock crowing. He thought of Inspector Starks at the wheel of his Sierra outside the lych gate, waiting for him to appear, accompanied by Palmer.

Robeson yawned. It had been a hard grind to tie up his case. Enthusiasm and adrenalin had carried him through. Now thirty hours without sleep was beginning to tell. He repeated, 'Come along, Mr Palmer.'

'I chucked 'er down the 'ole. Went down ladder an' covered 'er up.'

'All right, Mr Palmer.' Robeson went to take his arm and lift him up.

Palmer shook him off. 'Then 'e come back Friday. The dirty bugger. I dunno 'ow 'e ever 'ad neck enough to show 'is face 'ere again, I don't.' Palmer's red face deepened, he wiped his lips with the back of his hand. 'But every day that 'e come I asked 'im, "Where's yer whore then, Billy?" Put the wind up 'is sails I did. He'd go white round 'is gills 'e would.' Palmer hesitated. 'An' on Sunday I saw 'im moochin' round 'ere 'fore 'e went in to service. I said to 'im, I said, "What you done with yer whore, then, Billy? You dropped 'er bloody earrings. I've stuck 'em in yer jacket".' Palmer gave a malevolent chuckle. 'Put the fear of God in 'im, that did, the dirty bugger.'

Robeson put his hands gently but firmly on Palmer's arm to lever him up. But the man, like a little tub with an Edam cheese face, whose love for his holy garden had become fanatical, stood up, making no attempt to resist.

Later, Robeson found the Incident Room almost cleared of desks, files and maps. With a tired grin he accepted congratulations from Sergeant Mills. 'Thanks, Roger. But you know damn well it's team work. Reckon you all deserve a commend. I shall see the Chief and have a word.'

'Sir,' Mills said. 'About Slimbo Ferris. I know it makes no odds now. But that Sony cassette was taken to his shop by a Mrs Thomas.'

Robeson shrugged. It didn't matter. He'd got his man.

'That's who Fred Palmer lives with, sir,' Mills enlarged, sounding pleased to be helpful right to the end.

'I know, Roger. A little bird told me. She's Palmer's sister.'

'And *she's* got grey hair,' Mills added.

Robeson supposed it was she who had wasted her time cleaning that Sony. But her brother had signed his name that he had been fairly interviewed, and his prints on the form matched those on Ginger Retter's ladder.

Robeson gathered some files. He guessed that after Palmer had used the ladder to go down into Mrs Retter's grave and cover Kim Croft, he used it to reach the church window six feet from the ground. He had broken the glass right out, cleaned the surrounds, and concocted vandals to explain any signs of suspicious activity that might have been seen in the churchyard that night. Palmer wasn't too bright, but even he would have known he could not get through an aperture of seventeen by ten to plant a body in the coffin holding Mrs Retter. And Bible Billy had run off with the key of the church door in his pocket.

Robeson sighed loudly.

Mills said, 'Bet you're glad to be going home now, sir.'

'Dead right I am, Roger.'

With a grin Mills added, 'I bet you feel like celebrating.'

'Dead right again, Roger,' Robeson ran his fingers back through his curly brown hair, and his restless dark eyes shone in an answering, even wider grin. 'But not what you're thinking. I'm going home now for a bloody good sleep.'

20

Raine had never suffered personal tragedy. When her parents were killed she had been too young to understand that they were never coming home. By the time she realised, she had accepted living with Aunt Jo.

Now she watched Jeffrey, standing like a pillar of ice, looking out of the drawing-room window. She thought she knew his mind as well as she knew his six-foot frame, the square downright face, the well-shaped dark brows and smooth, firm chin. But since his return from the mortuary he seemed a stranger.

She wondered how long it would be before he spoke. She almost wished she had gone with him. He would know then that she shared at least some of his horror, if not quite the same personal grief.

She poured him a whisky. He waved it away. She replaced it on the small side table.

She went back to him and took his hand in hers. He didn't respond but she kept hold of his hand, willing him to know that she loved him and was there to help him to recover from the shock of this tragedy.

If only she had tried harder to understand Kim. If only she could have shown her more warmth and love. She had wanted to. Really wanted to.

But instead, too readily she had accepted it was too late to undo the lamentable results of Kim's lax upbringing. She had waited impatiently to hand over the responsibility for Kim to her father, Jeffrey.

Outside, the September day was calm. Gorse and heather still coloured the common. Some late holidaymakers walked hand in hand towards the trees. A string of riders on horseback followed bridle paths beside the scrub. Beyond them, in the distance, the sea was smooth, the colour of steel. A large tanker, about ten miles out on the horizon, moved slowly down the Channel.

She thought, life still goes on. Just the same. It doesn't stop, or change, while those in trouble picked themselves up. She supposed there would always be murder, wickedness, and grief...

Then so too, by that reckoning, she consoled herself as she glanced up at Jeffrey, there would still be, there must always be, goodness and love.

She held his hand more firmly.

She felt him move; release his hand. He lowered his face and put his cheek against hers. Then his arms were around her, holding her tightly.

She did not expect to be kissed. She would be patient. Let him recover slowly. But she knew, for certain now, this was the beginning of the new start that she and Jeffrey had been going to make.